MW00788602

DO YOU SPEAK TREE?

DO YOU SPEAK TREE?

Creative Director
Amelia Boscov

Writer
Josh Oaktree

Illustrator
Josiane Vlitos

Oak Tree Comics, Los Angeles

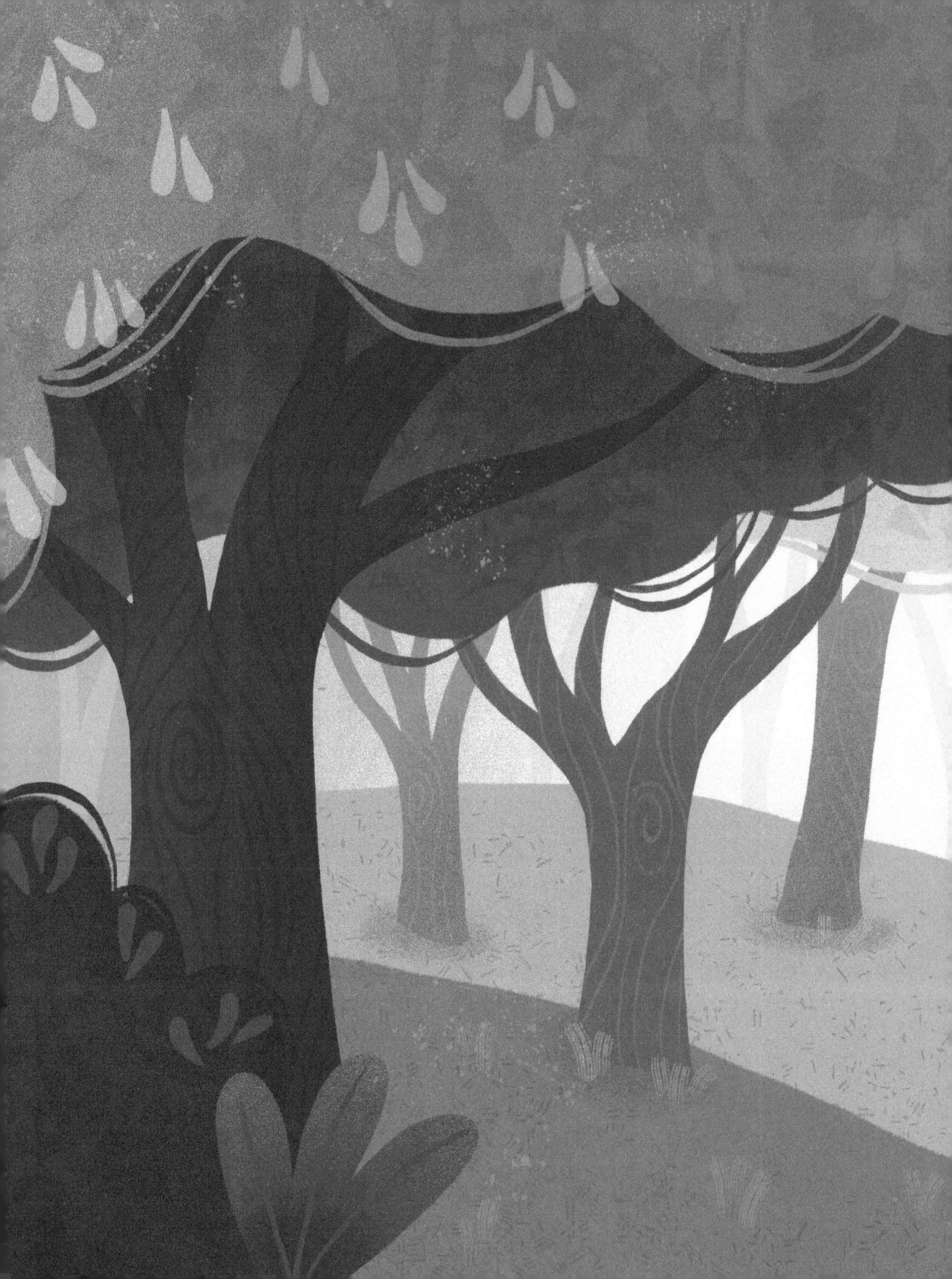

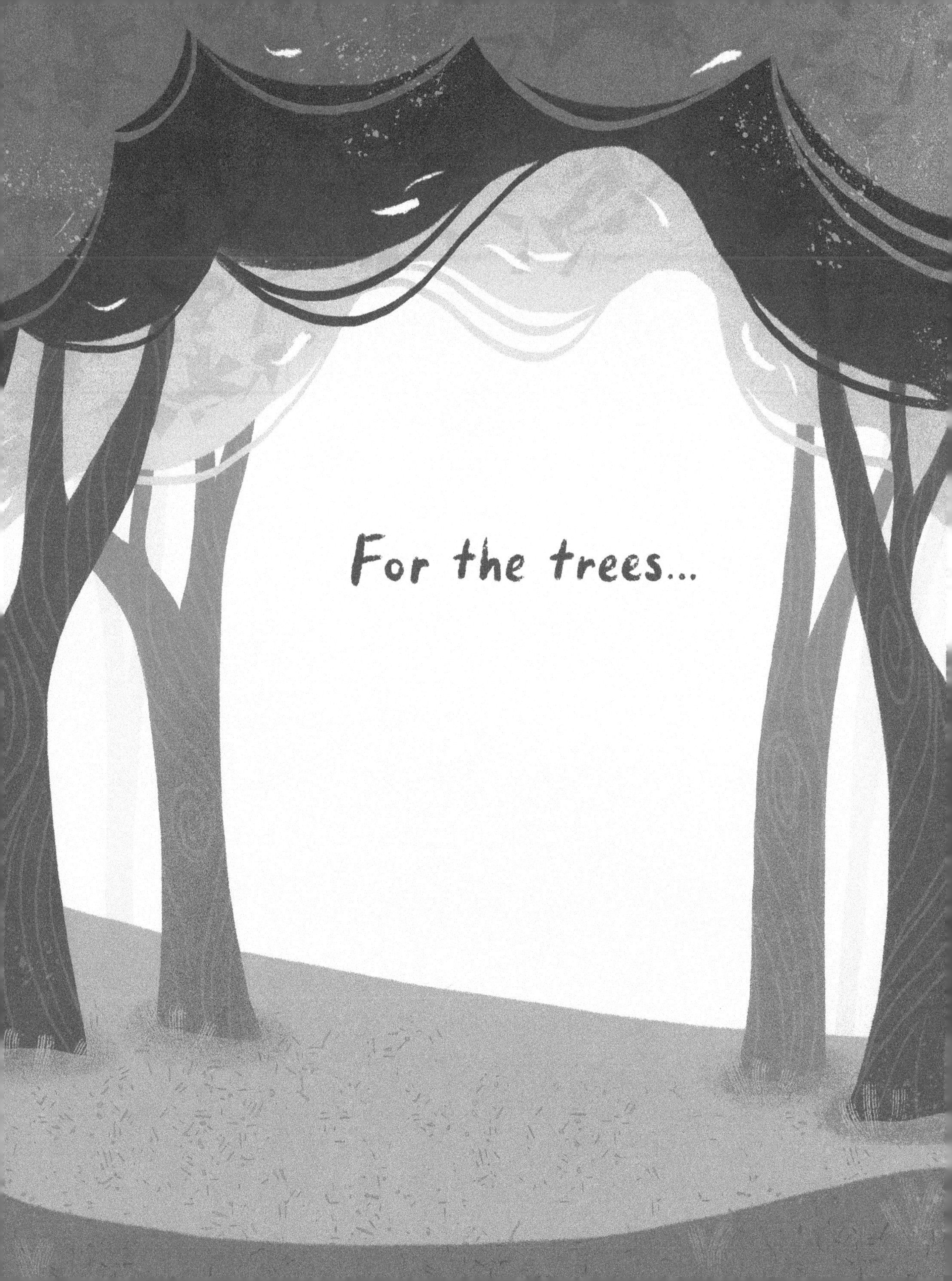

For the trees...

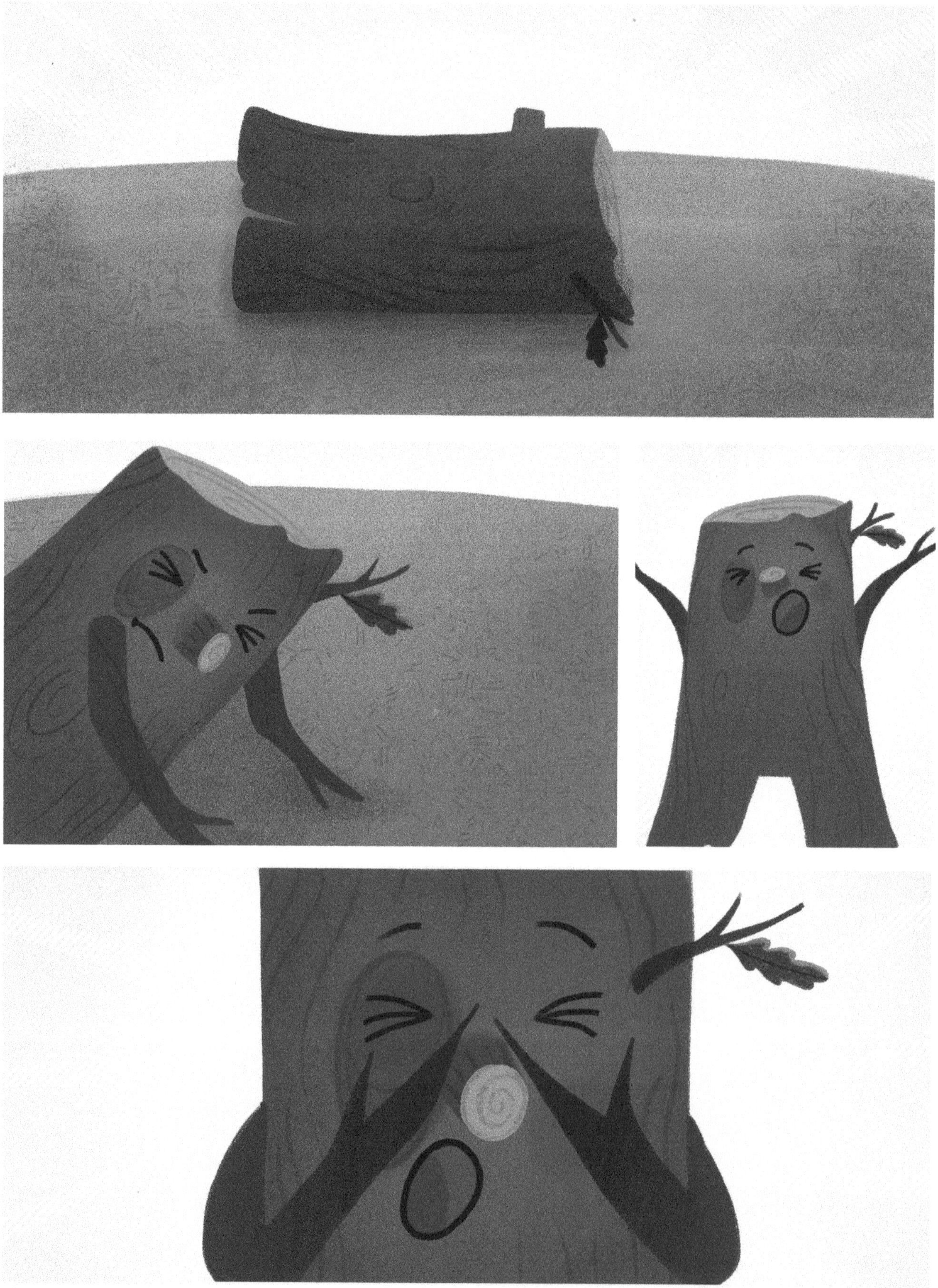

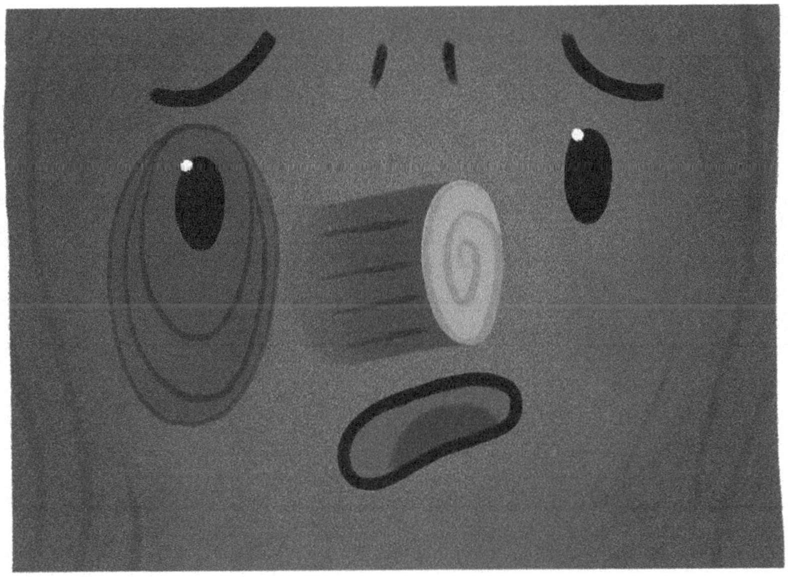

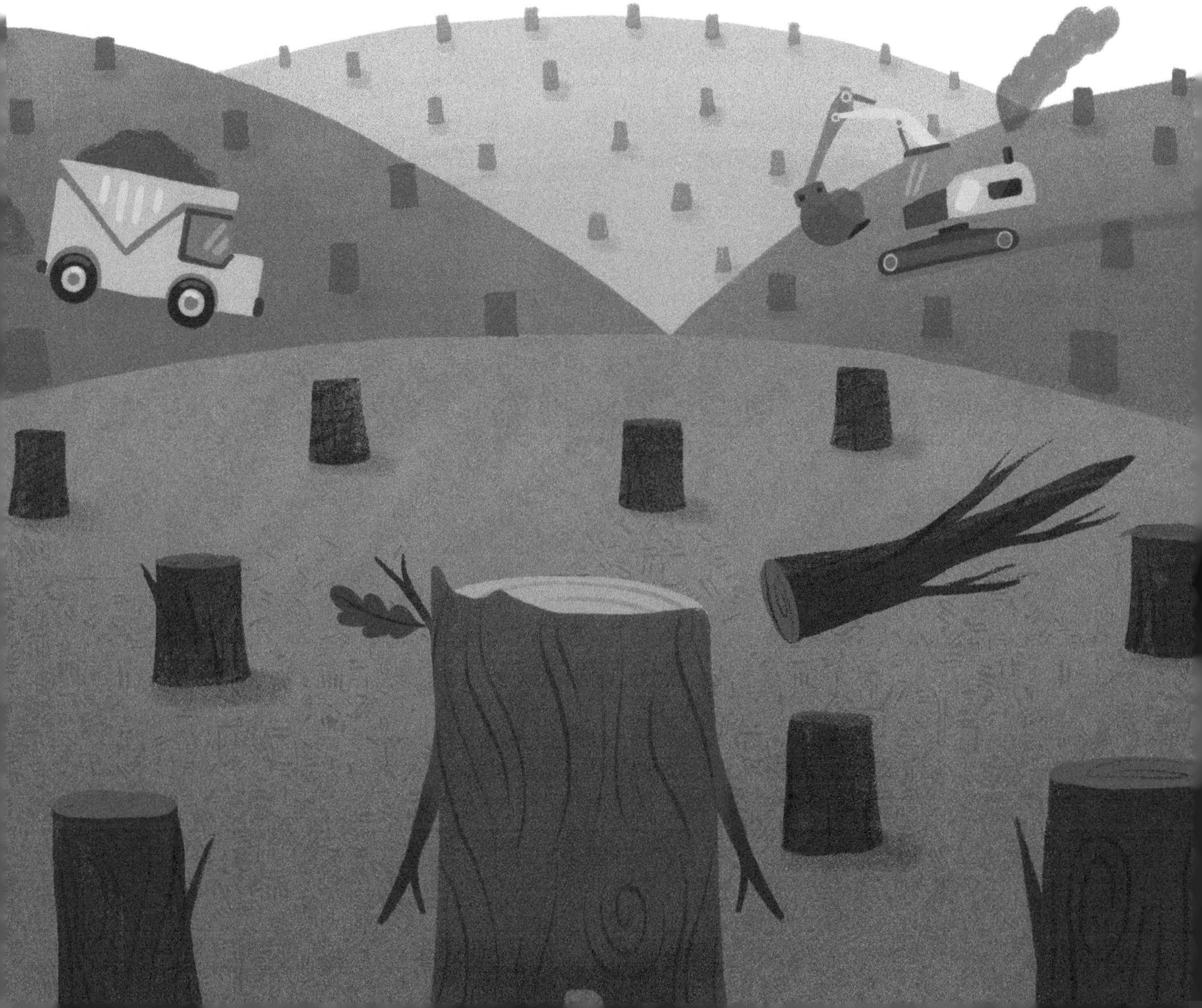

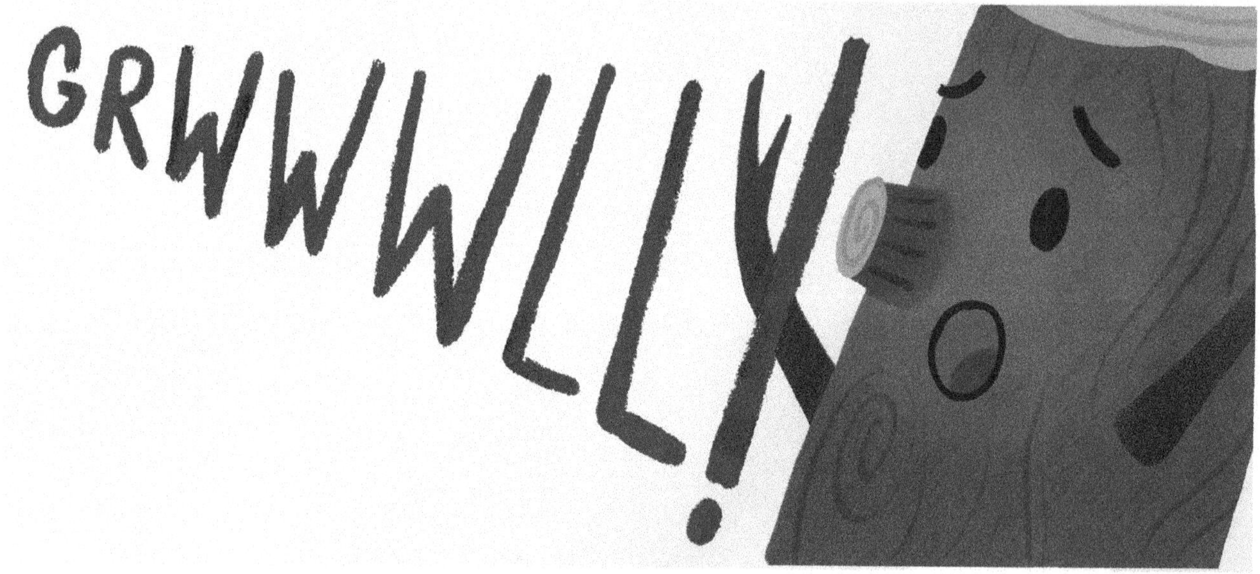
GRWWWLLLY!

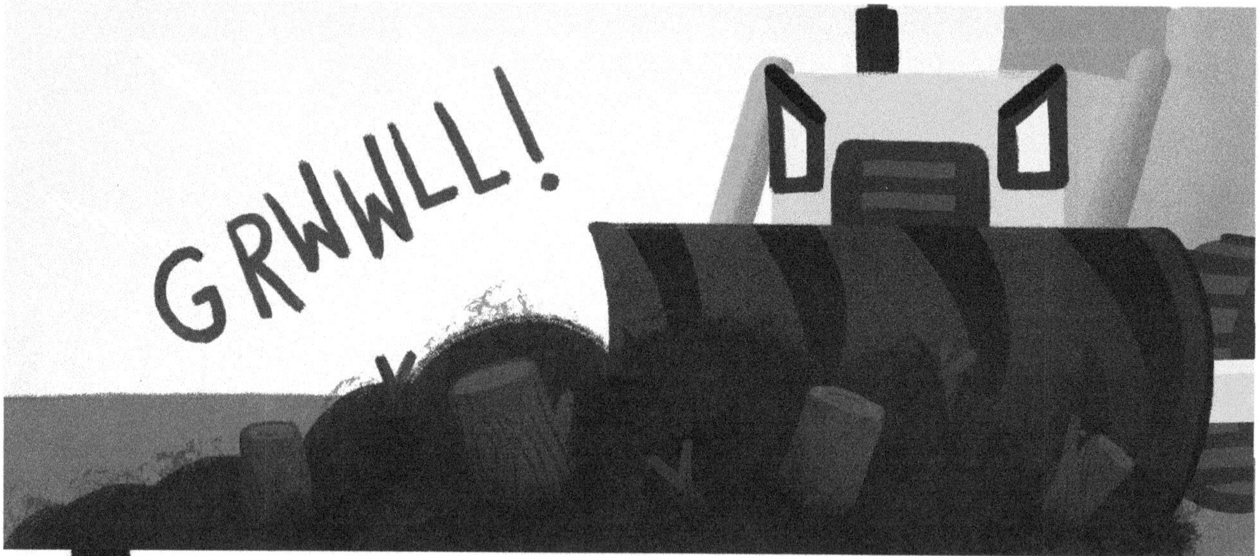
GRWWLL!

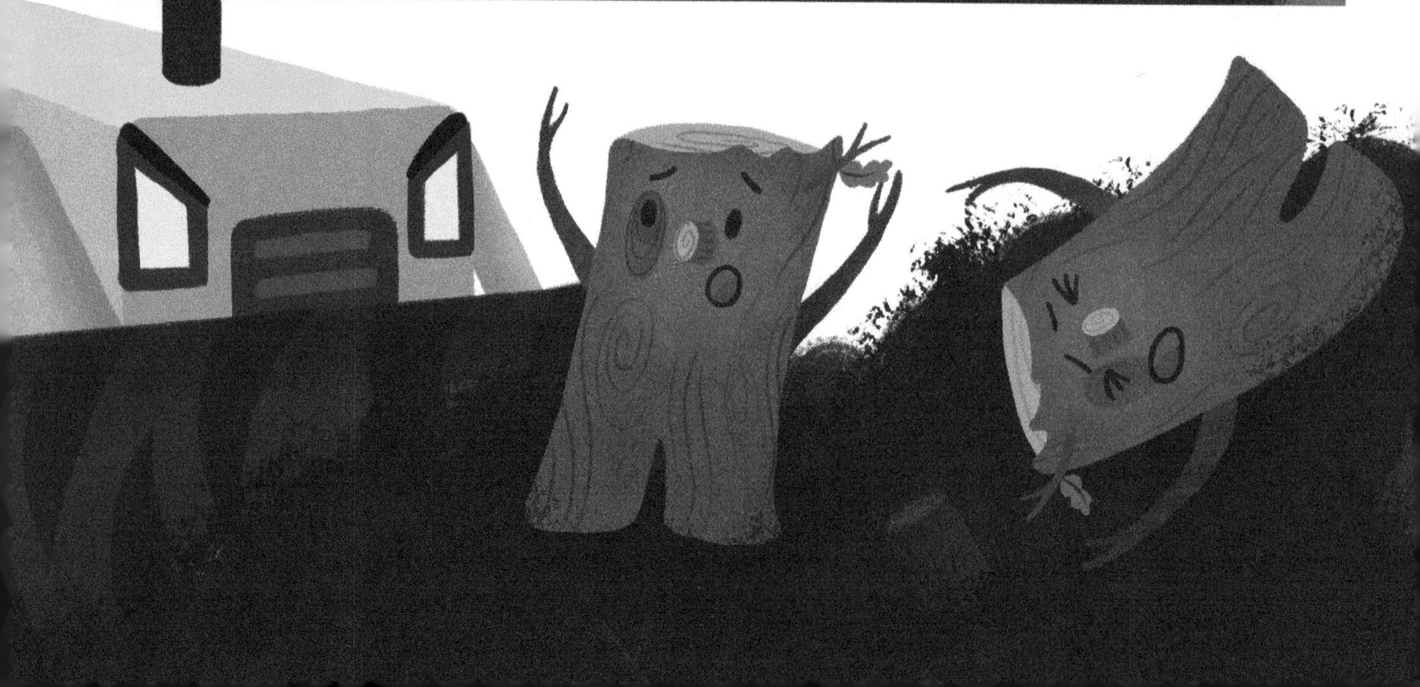

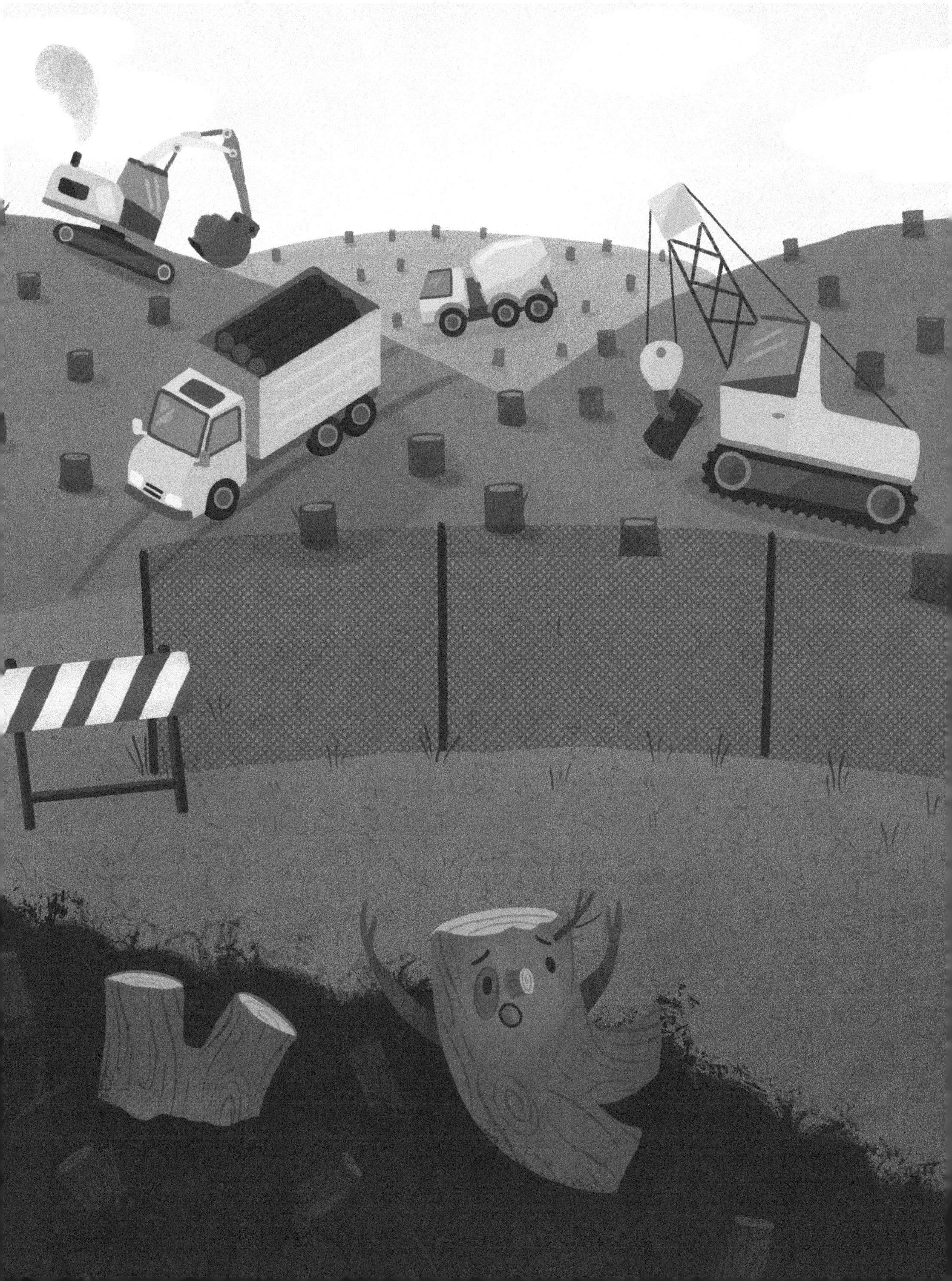

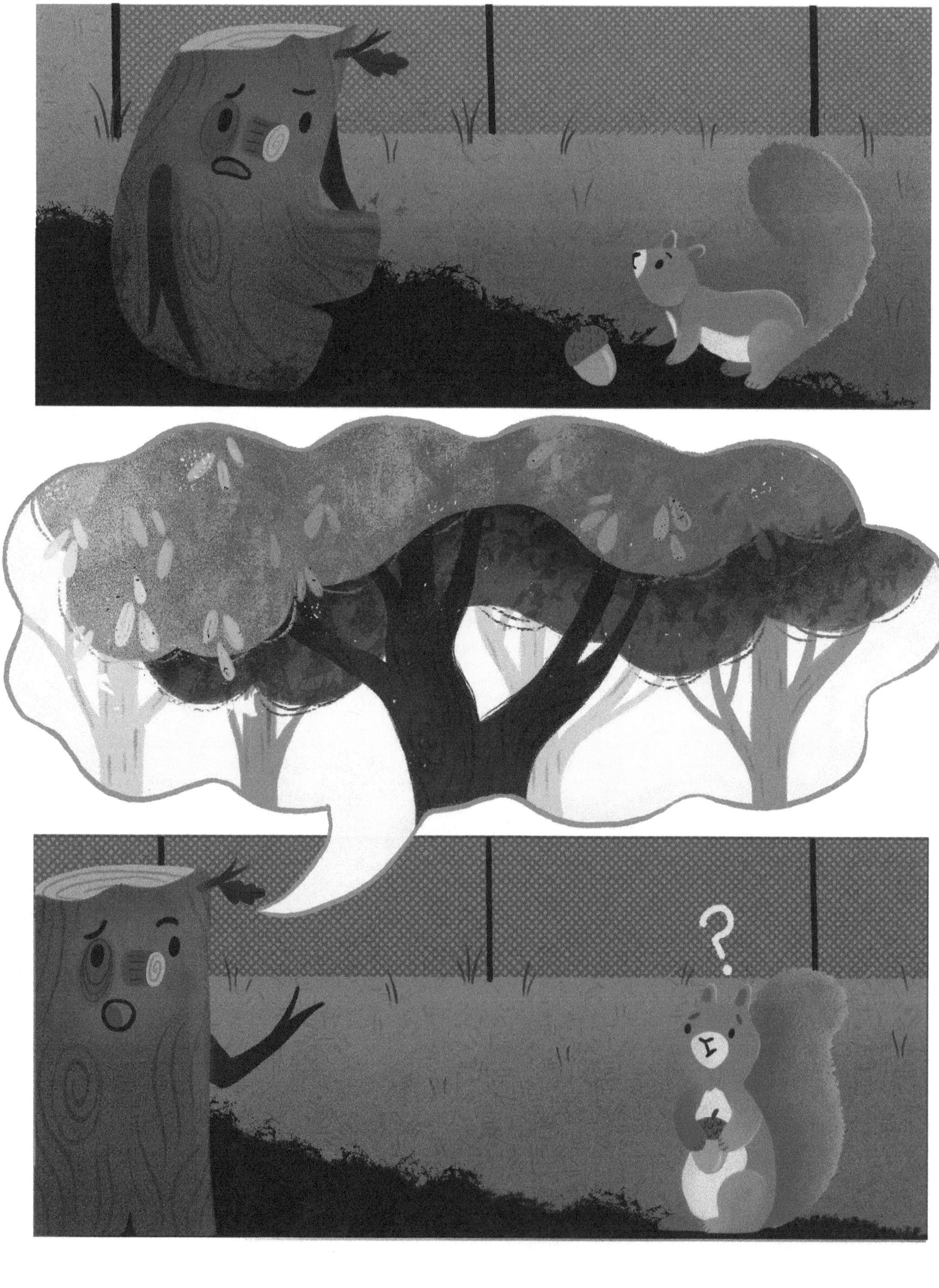
?

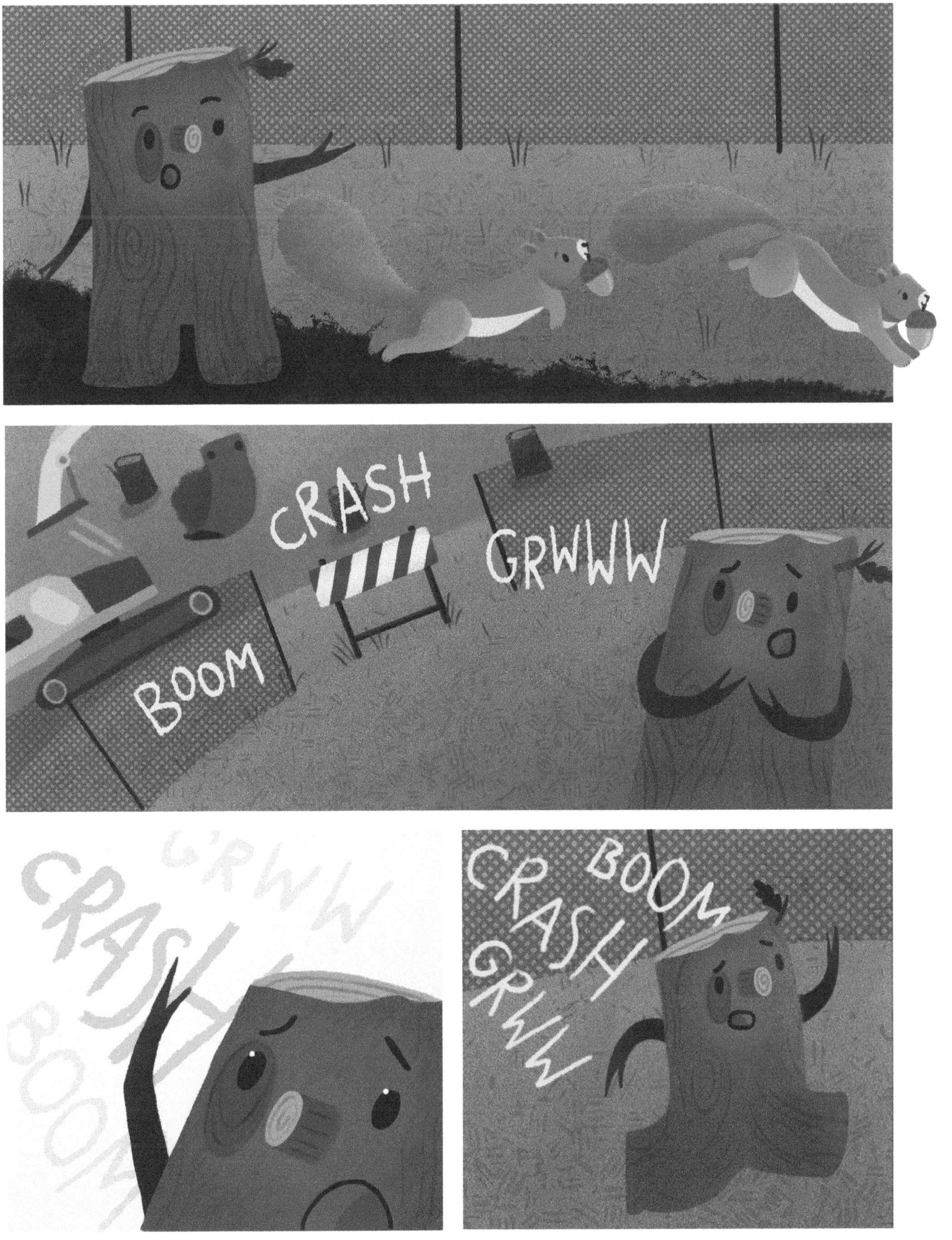
CRASH
GRWWW
BOOM
GRWW
CRASH
BOOM
BOOM
CRASH
GRWW

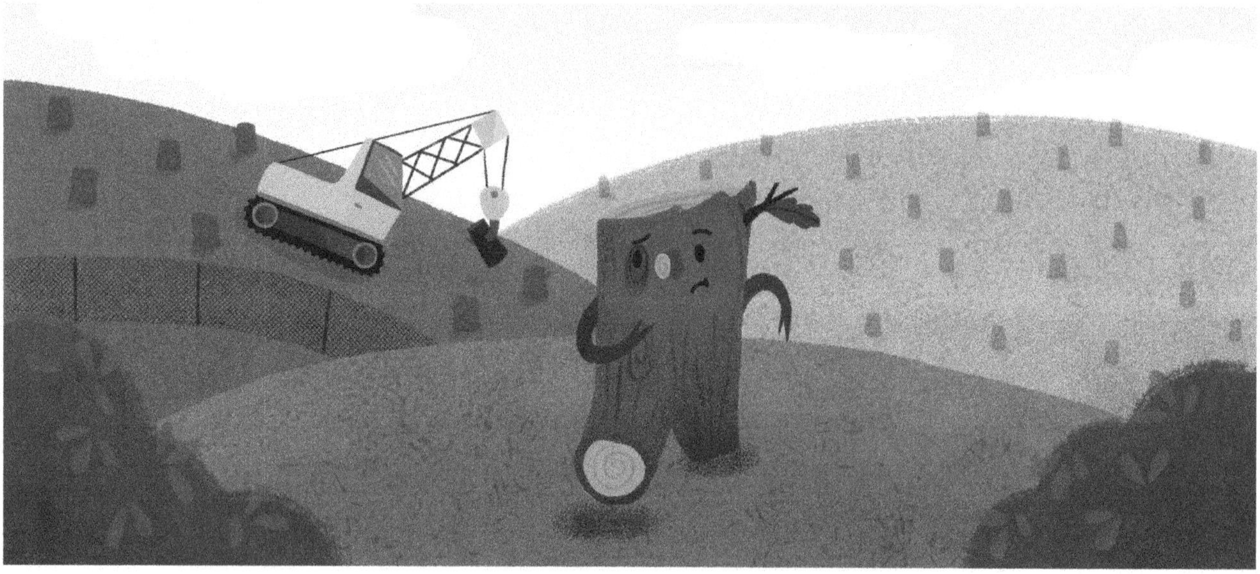

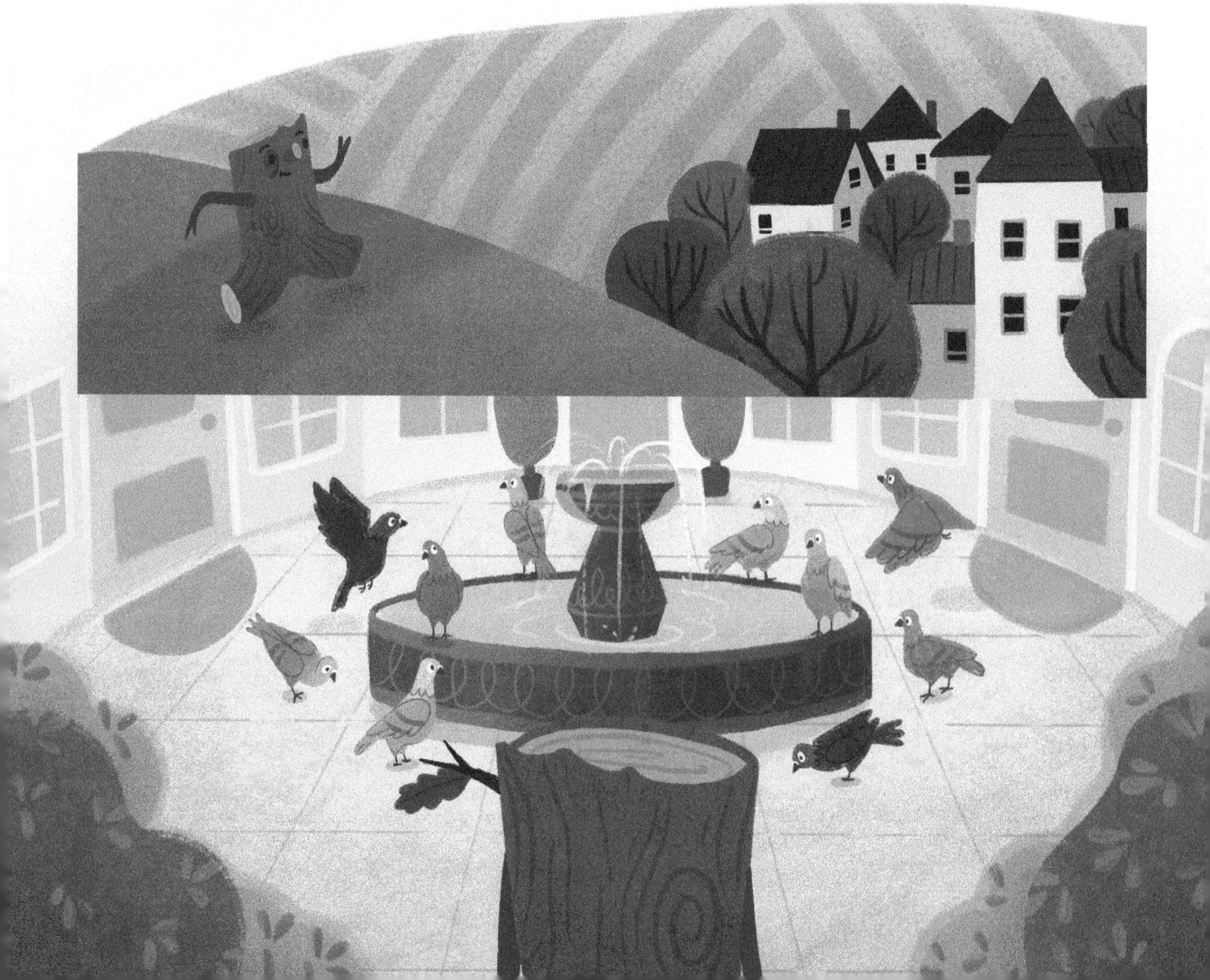

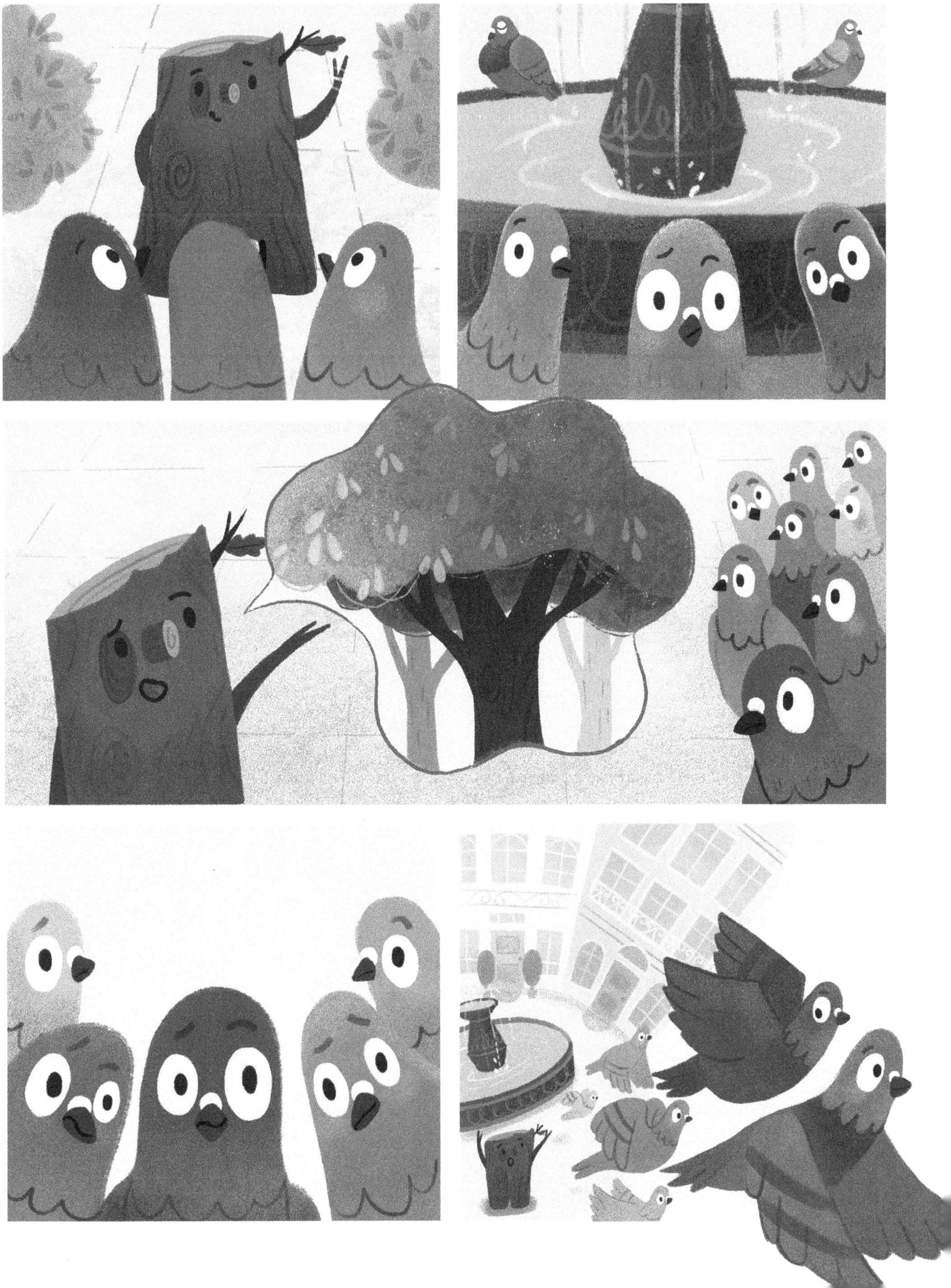

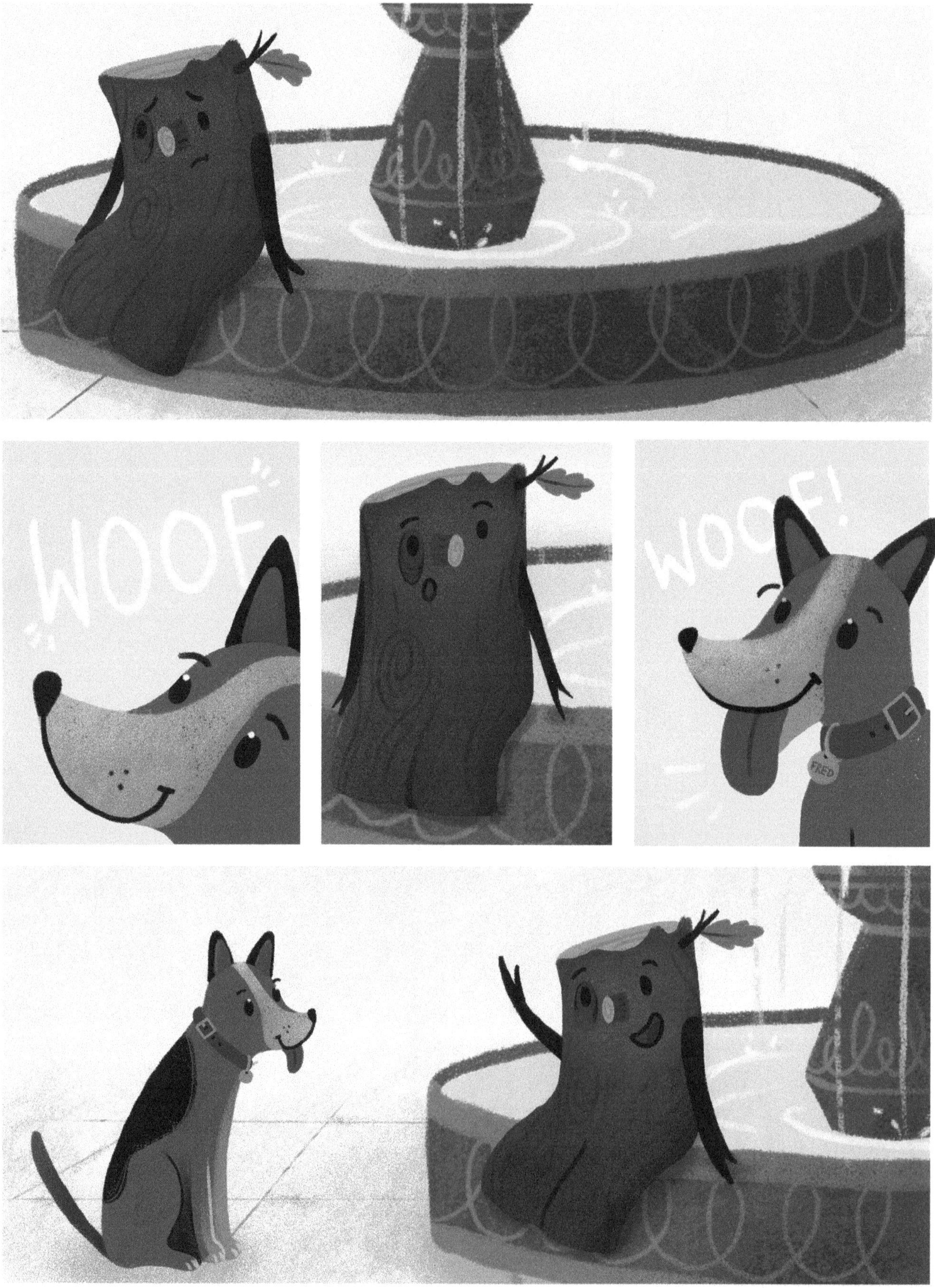
WOOF
WOOF!
FRED

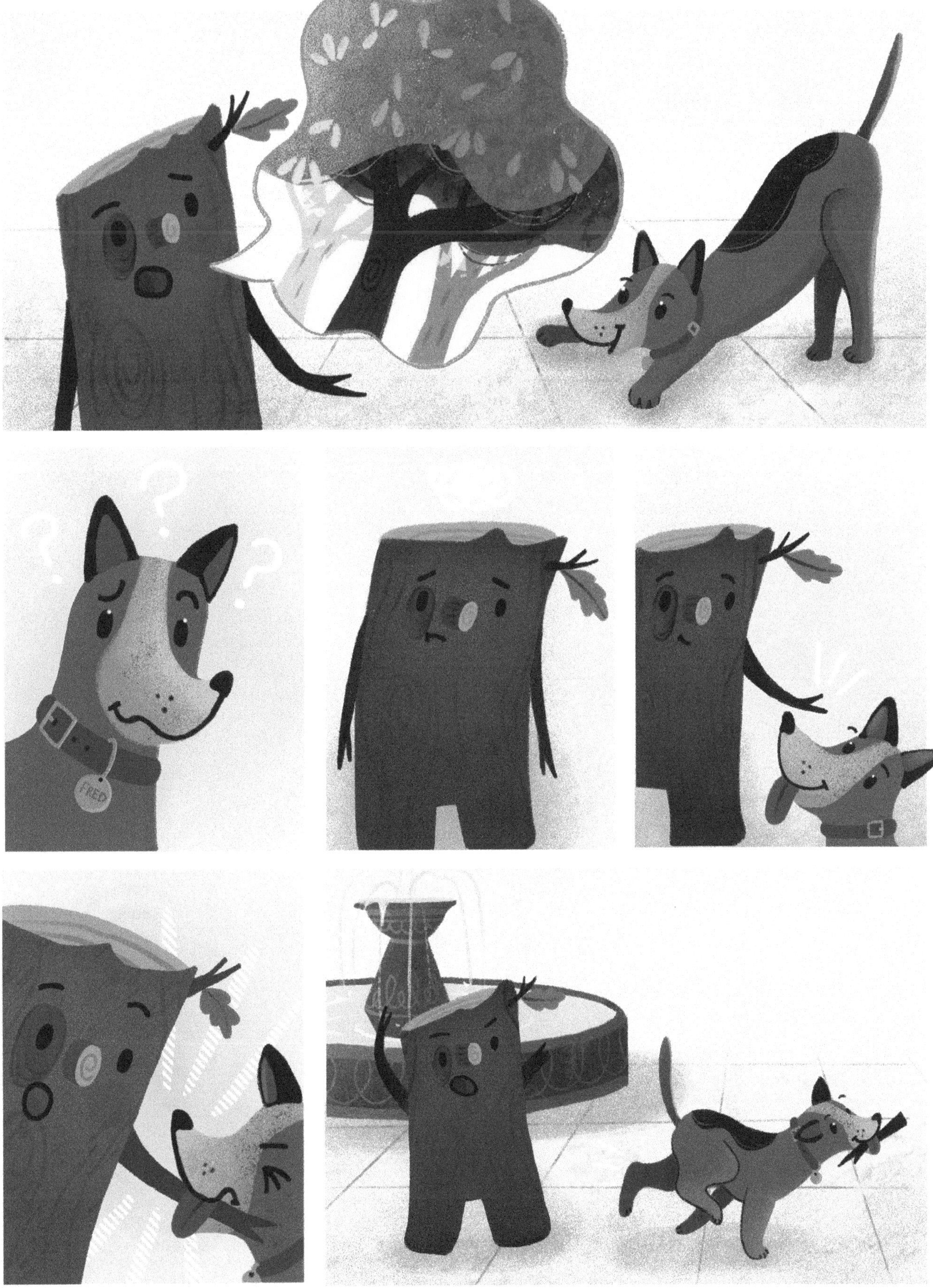
FRED

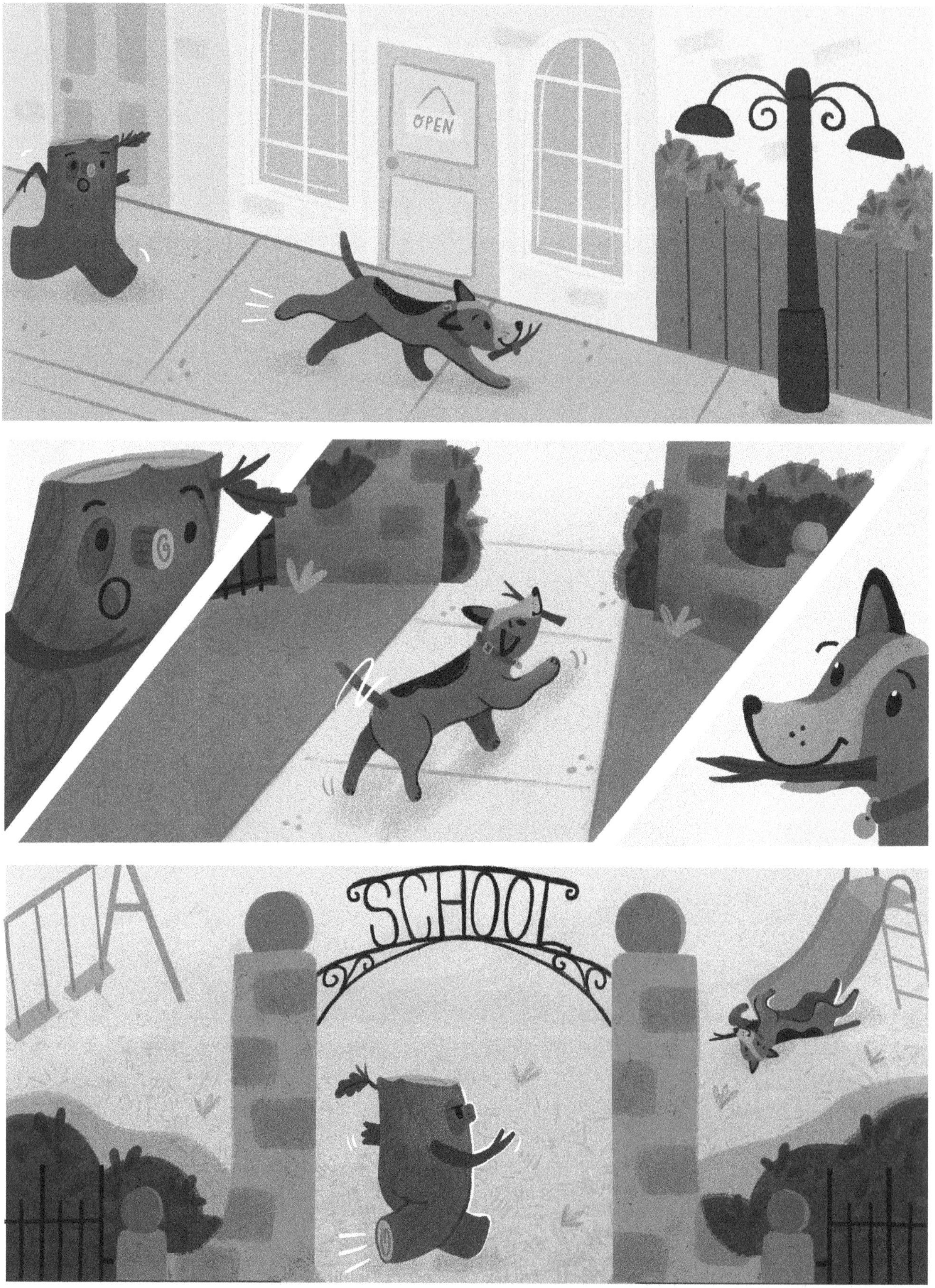
OPEN
SCHOOL

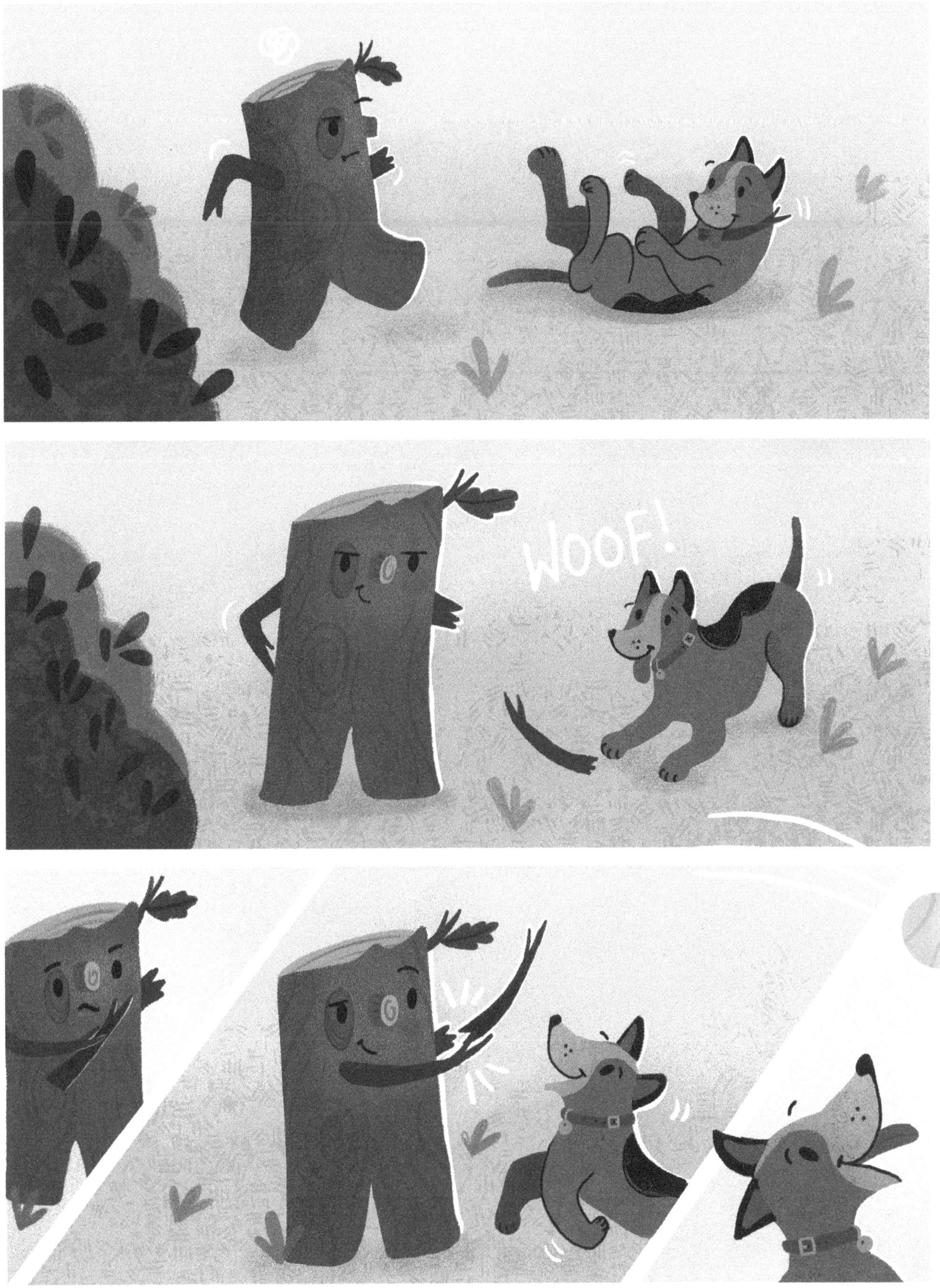
WOOF!

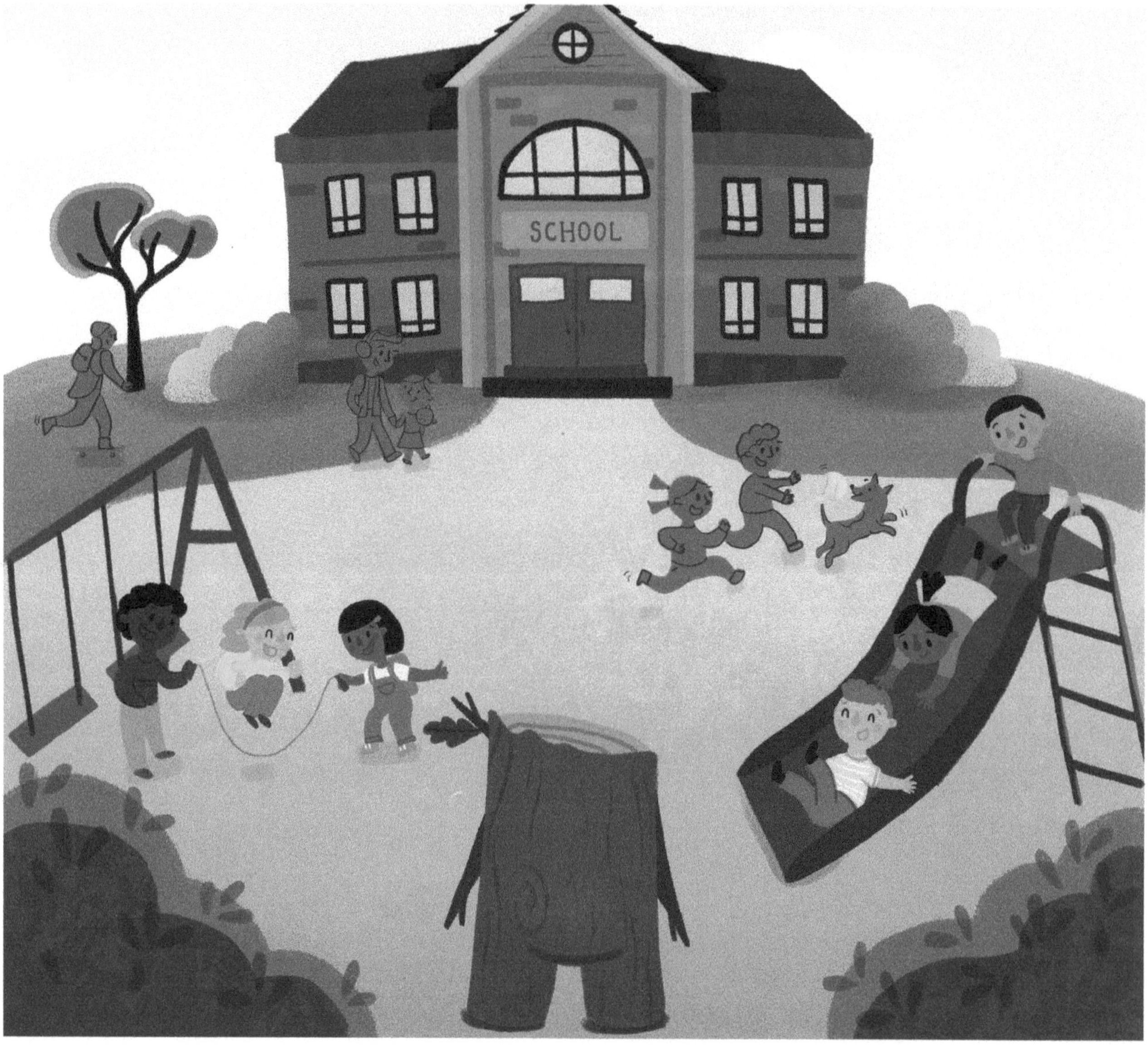
SCHOOL

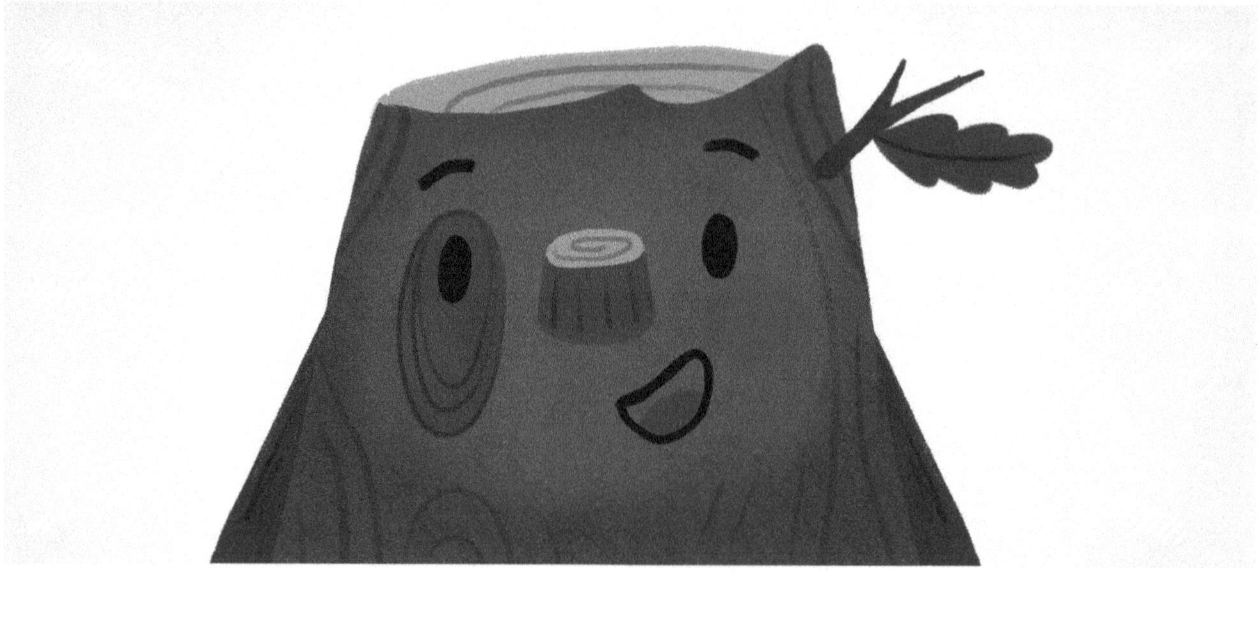

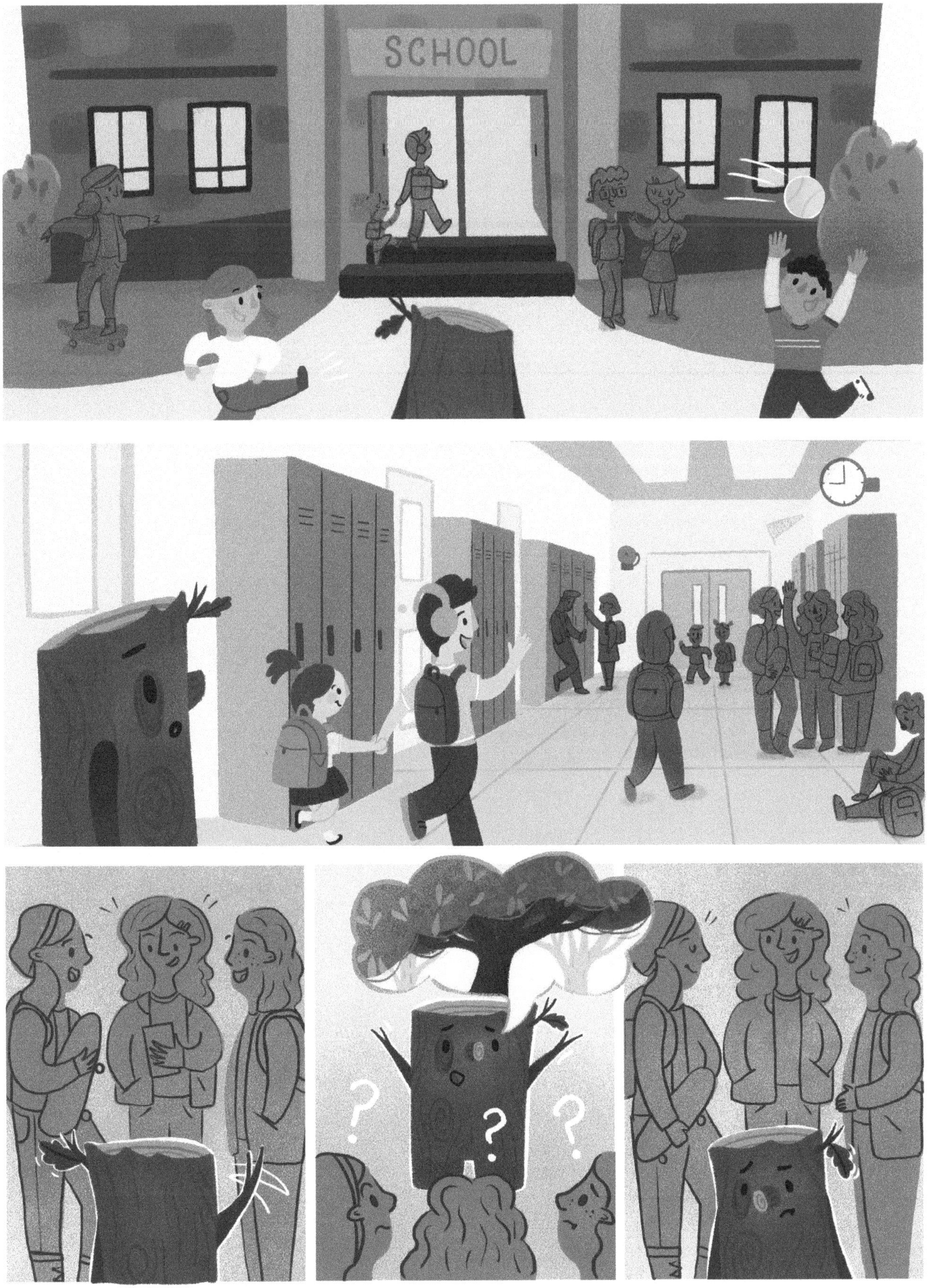
SCHOOL

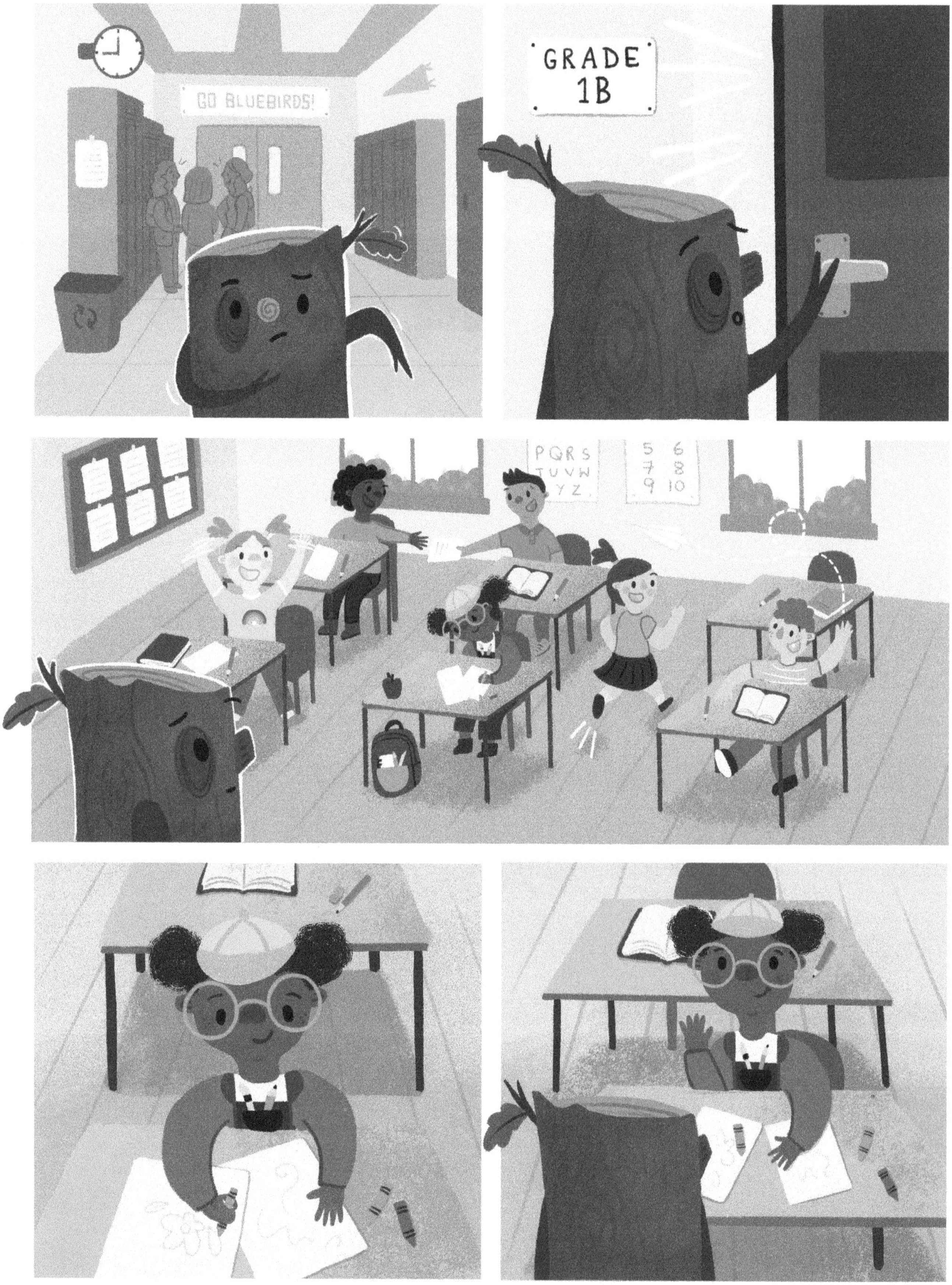
GO BLUEBIRDS!
GRADE 1B
PQRS
TUVW
YZ
5 6
7 8
9 10

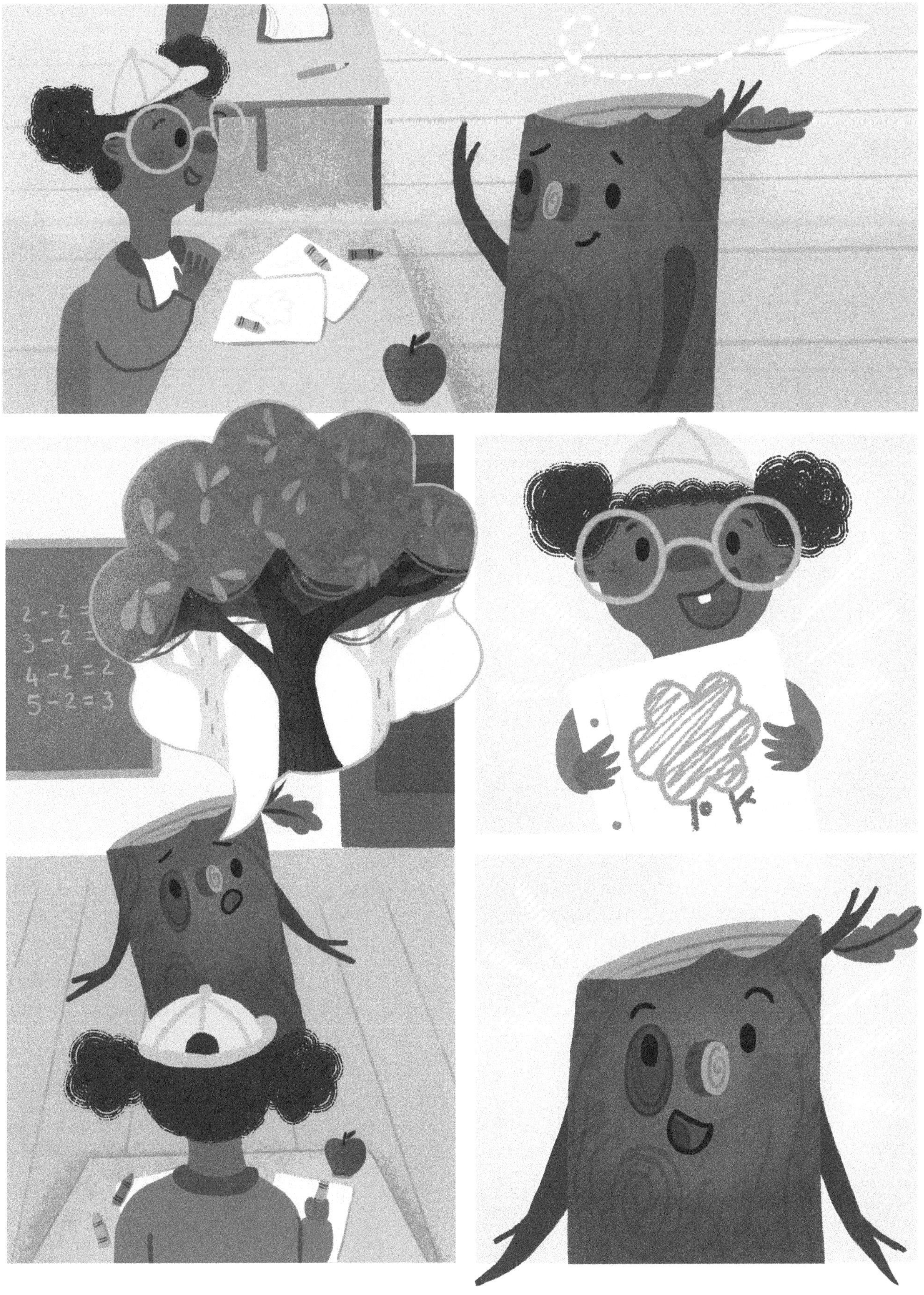
2 - 2 =
3 - 2 =
4 - 2 = 2
5 - 2 = 3

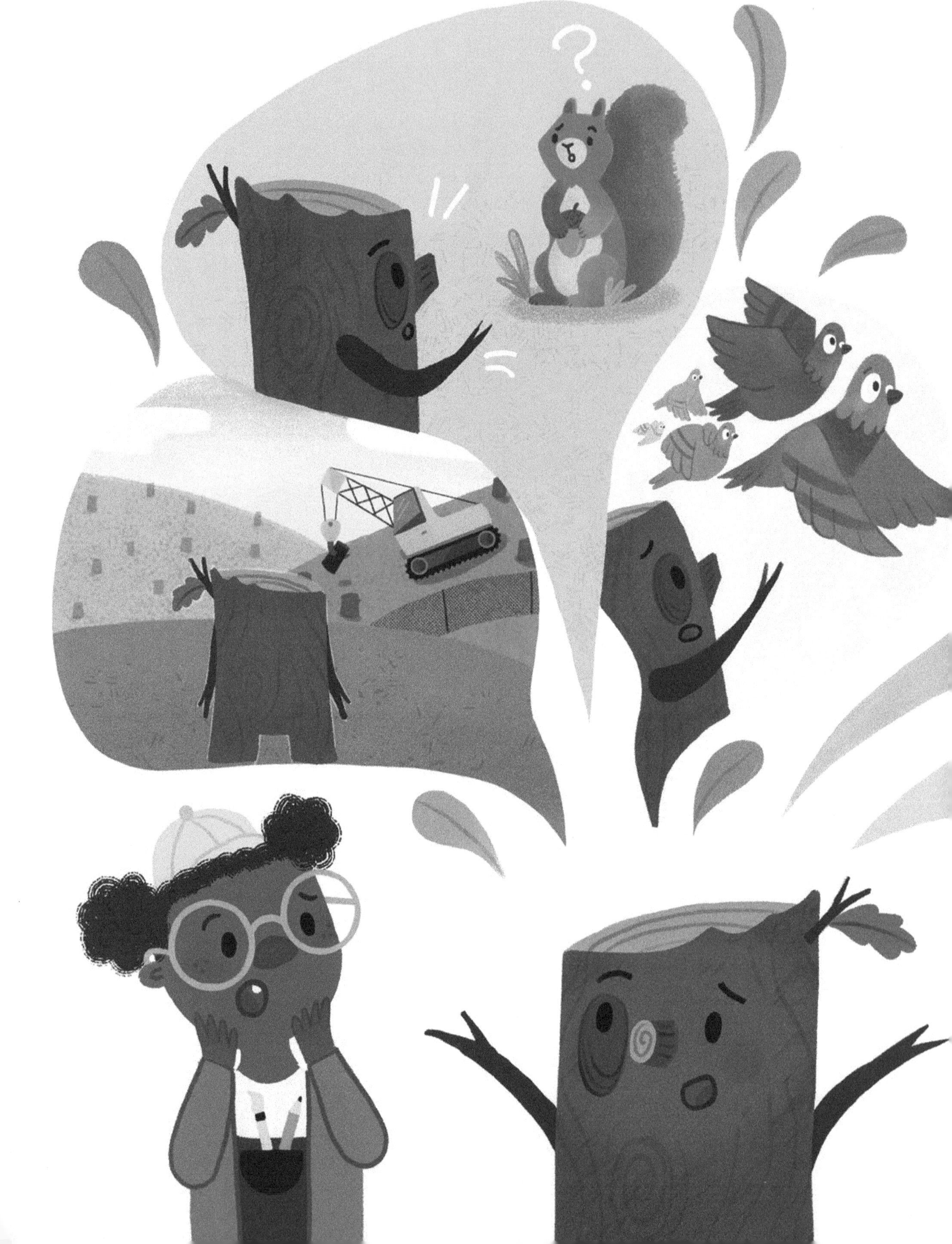

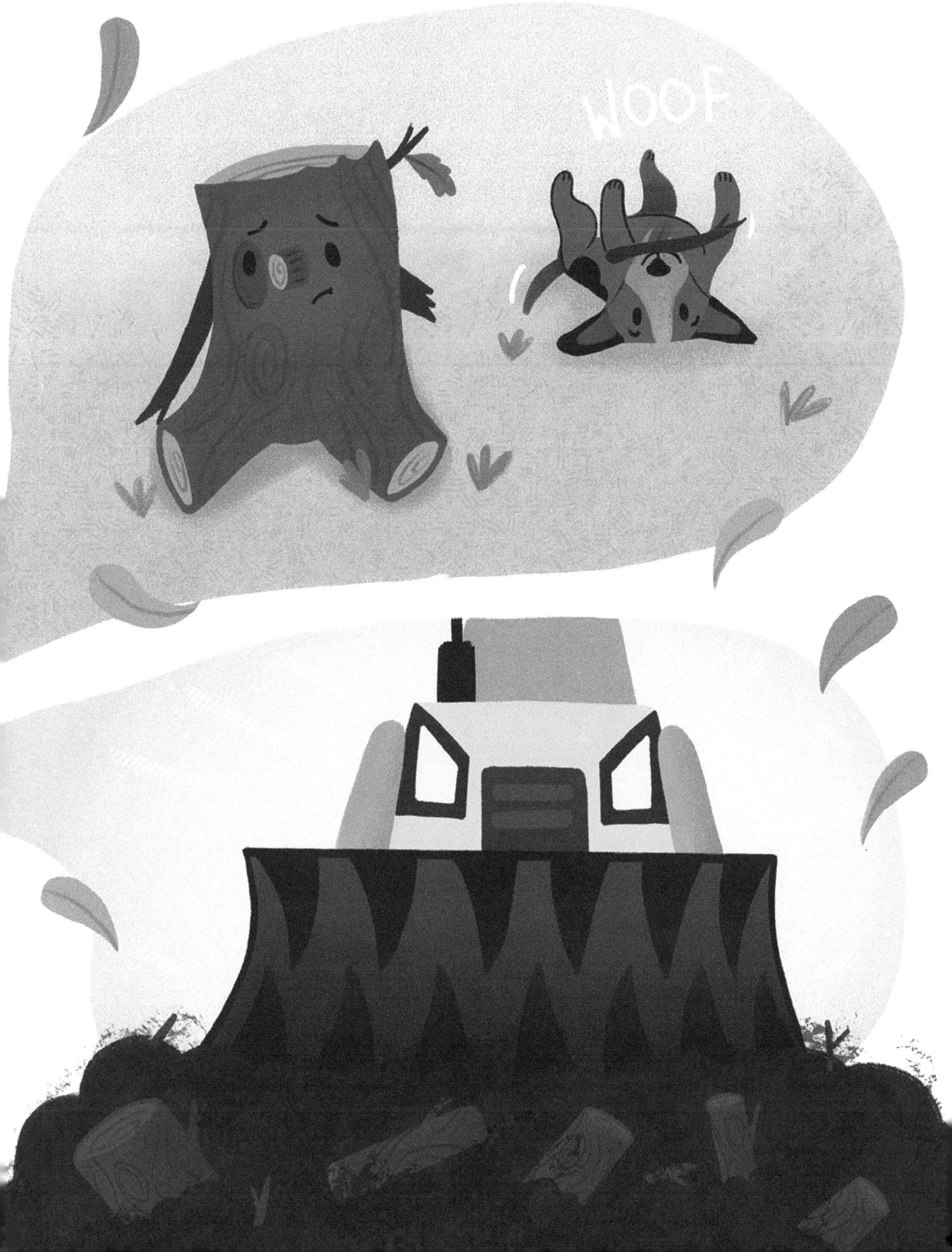
WOOF

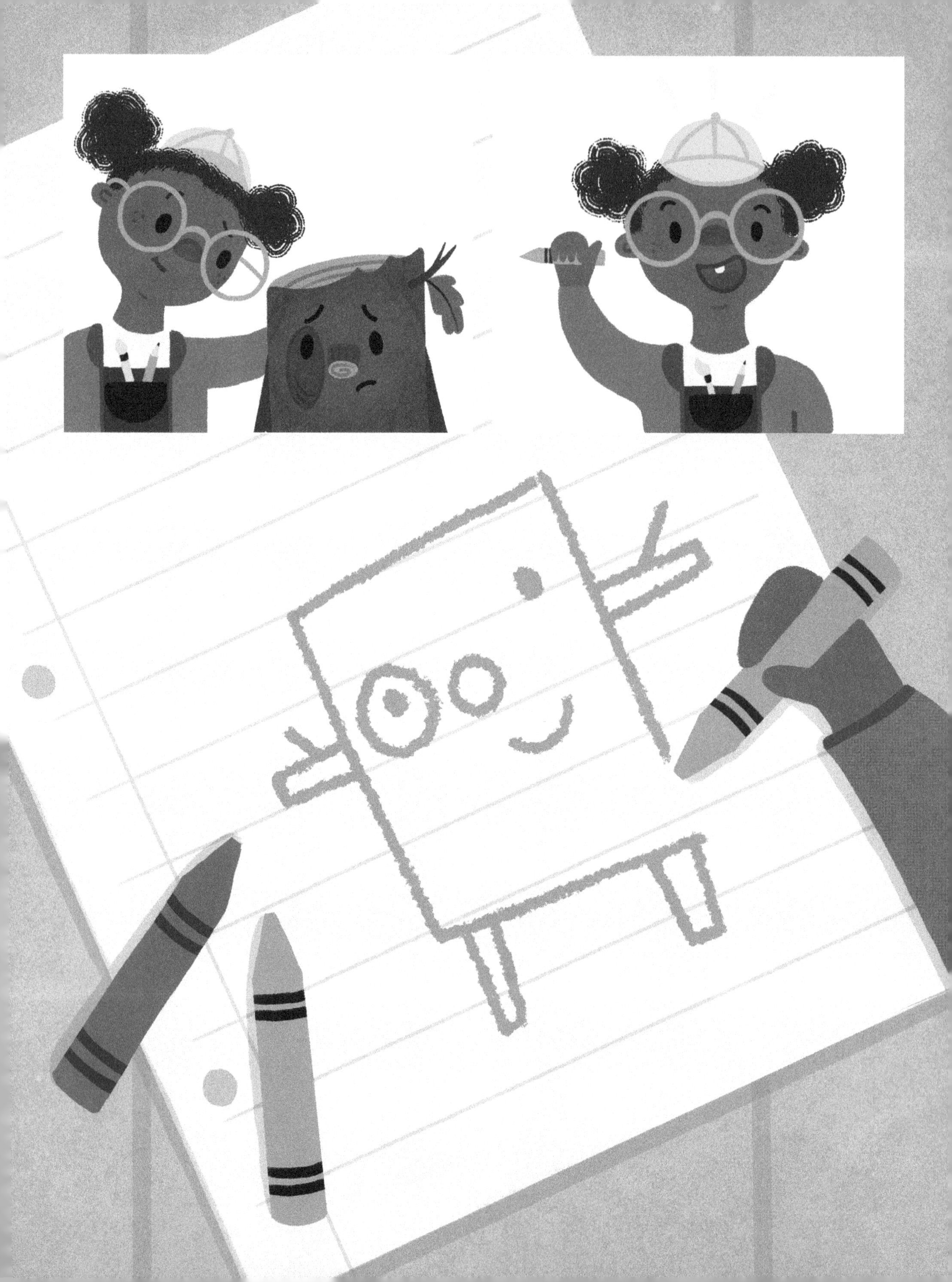

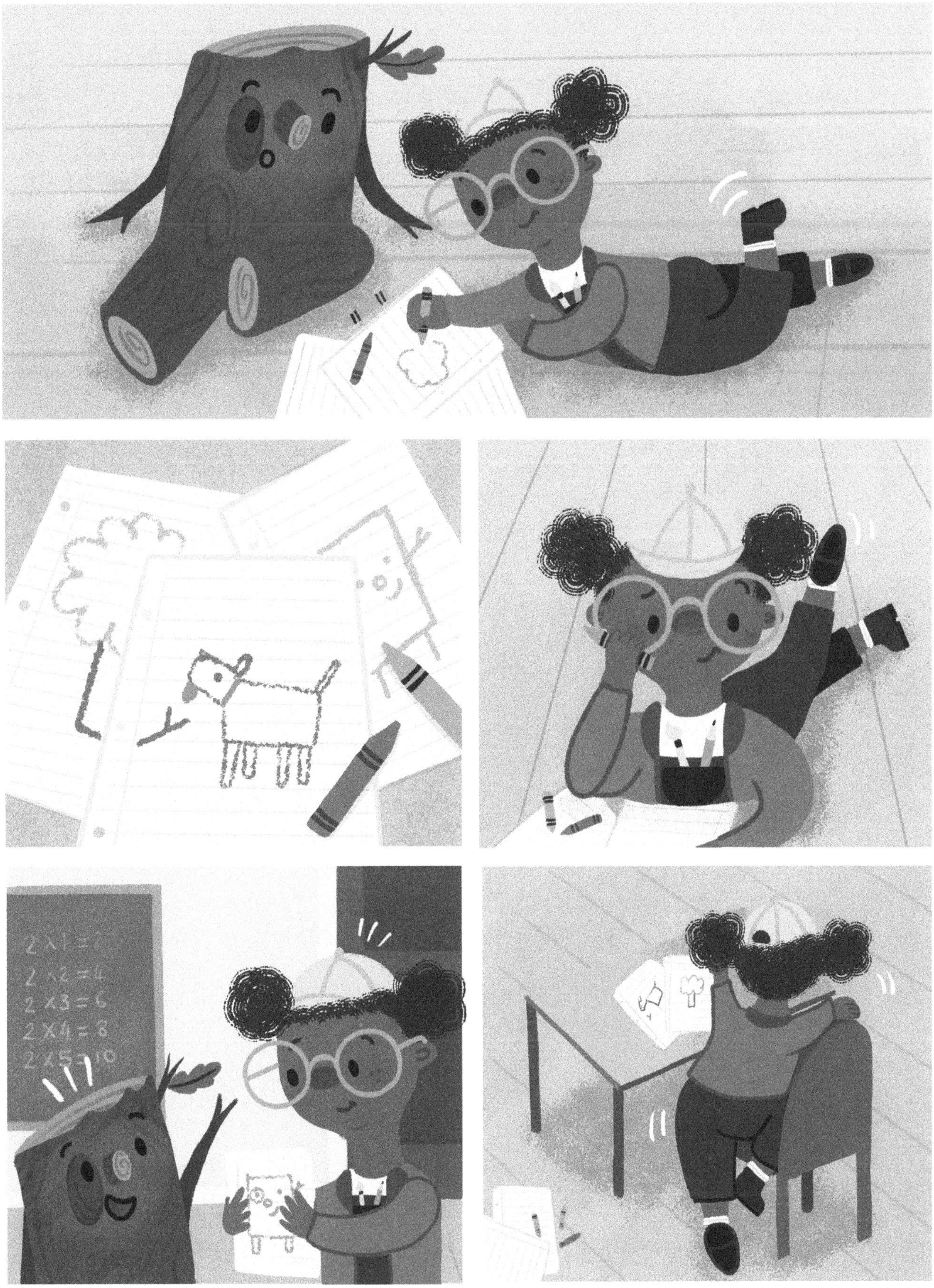
2 X 1 = 2
2 X 2 = 4
2 X 3 = 6
2 X 4 = 8
2 X 5 = 10

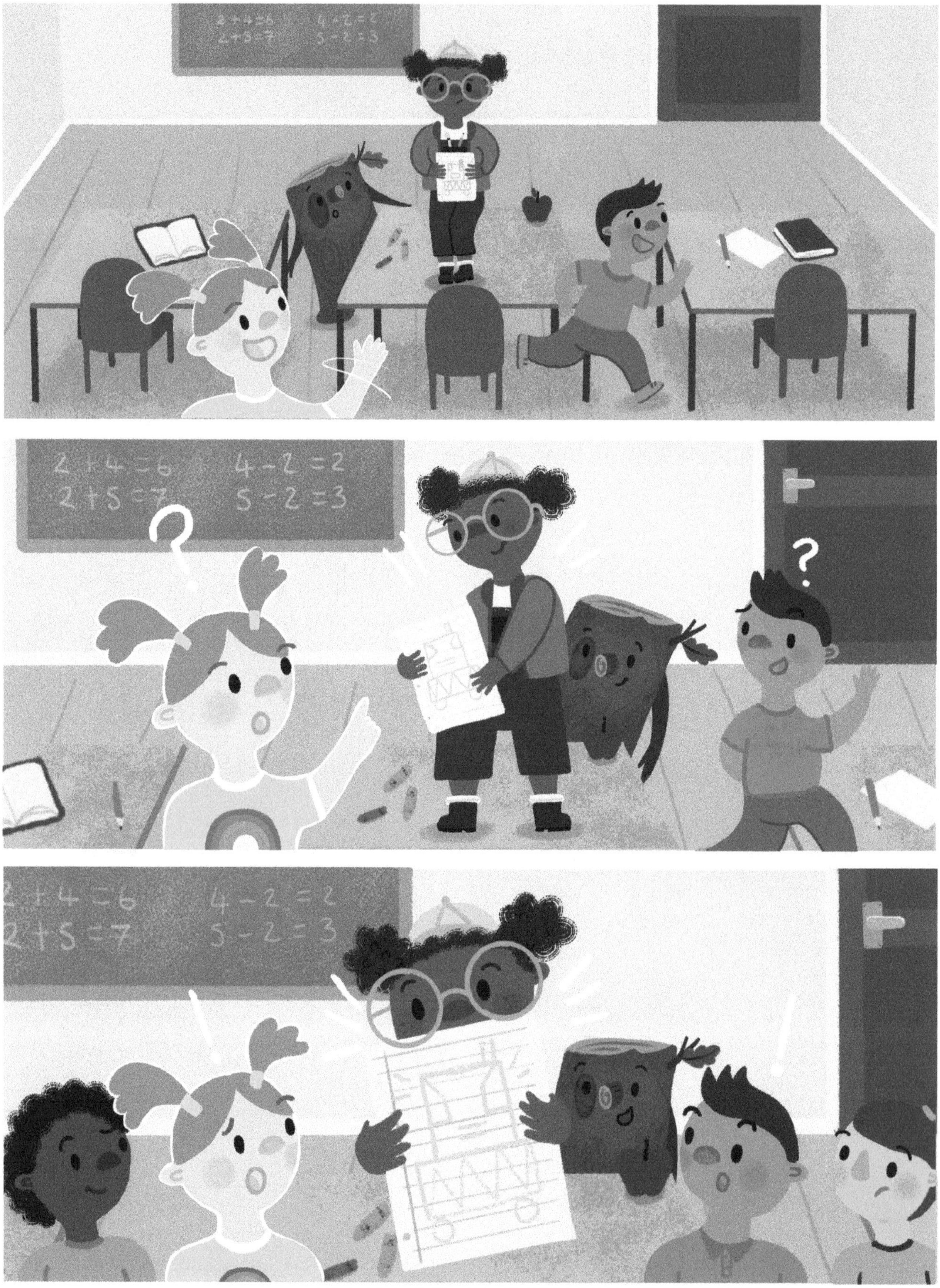
2+4=6
4-2=2
2+5=7
5-2=3

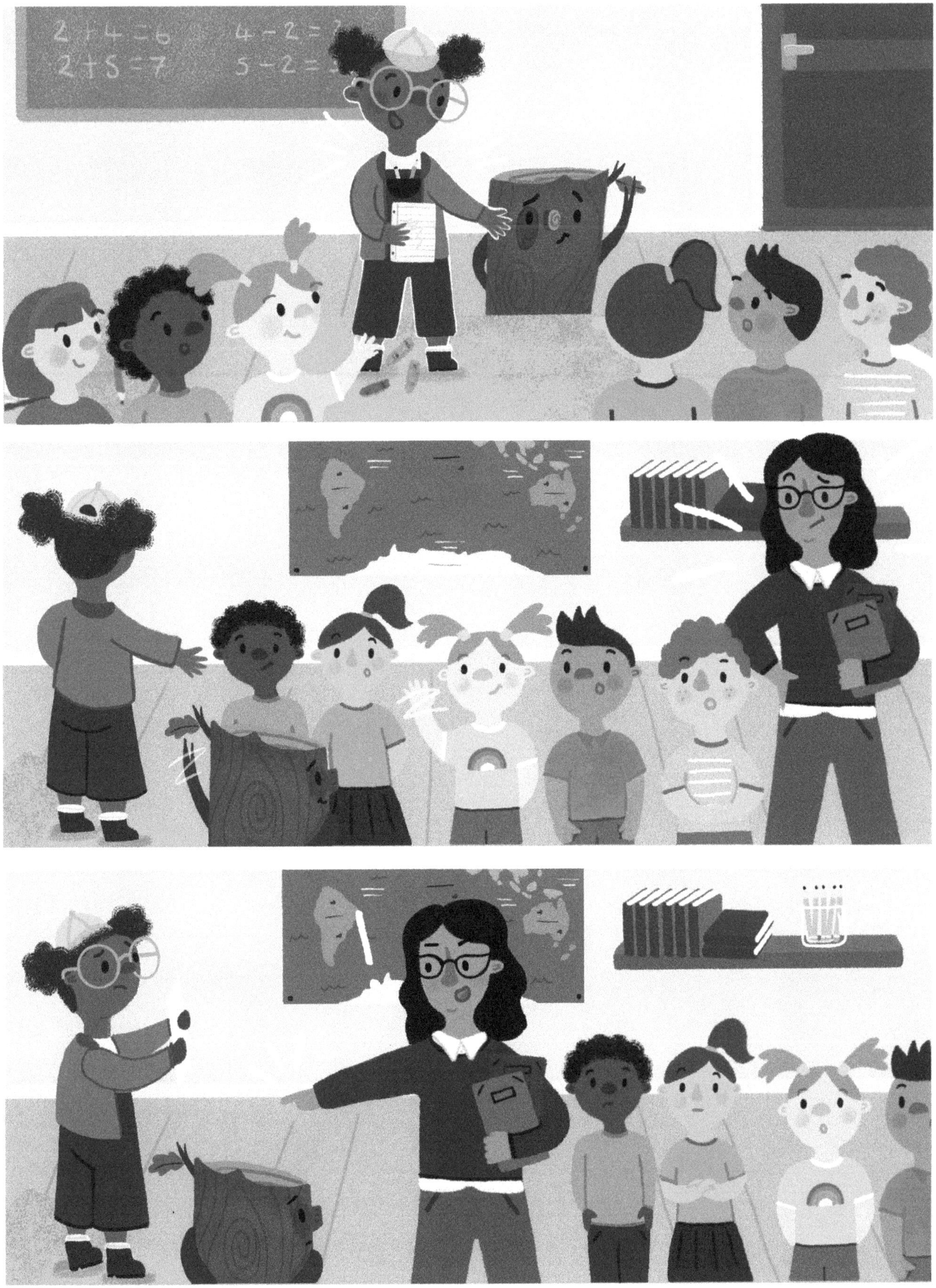
2 + 4 = 6
4 - 2 =
2 + 5 = 7
5 - 2 =

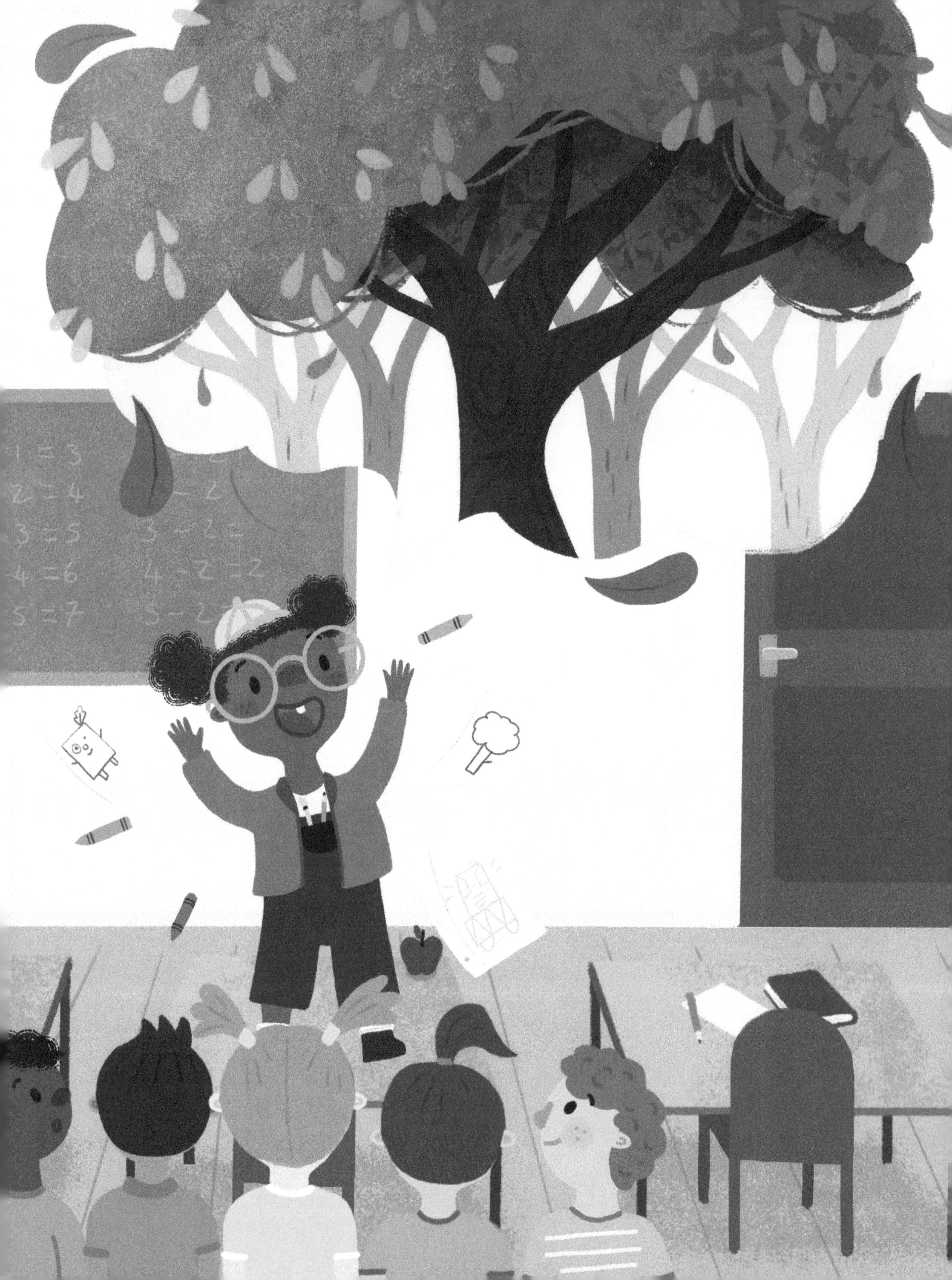
1 = 3
2 = 4
3 = 5
4 = 6
5 = 7

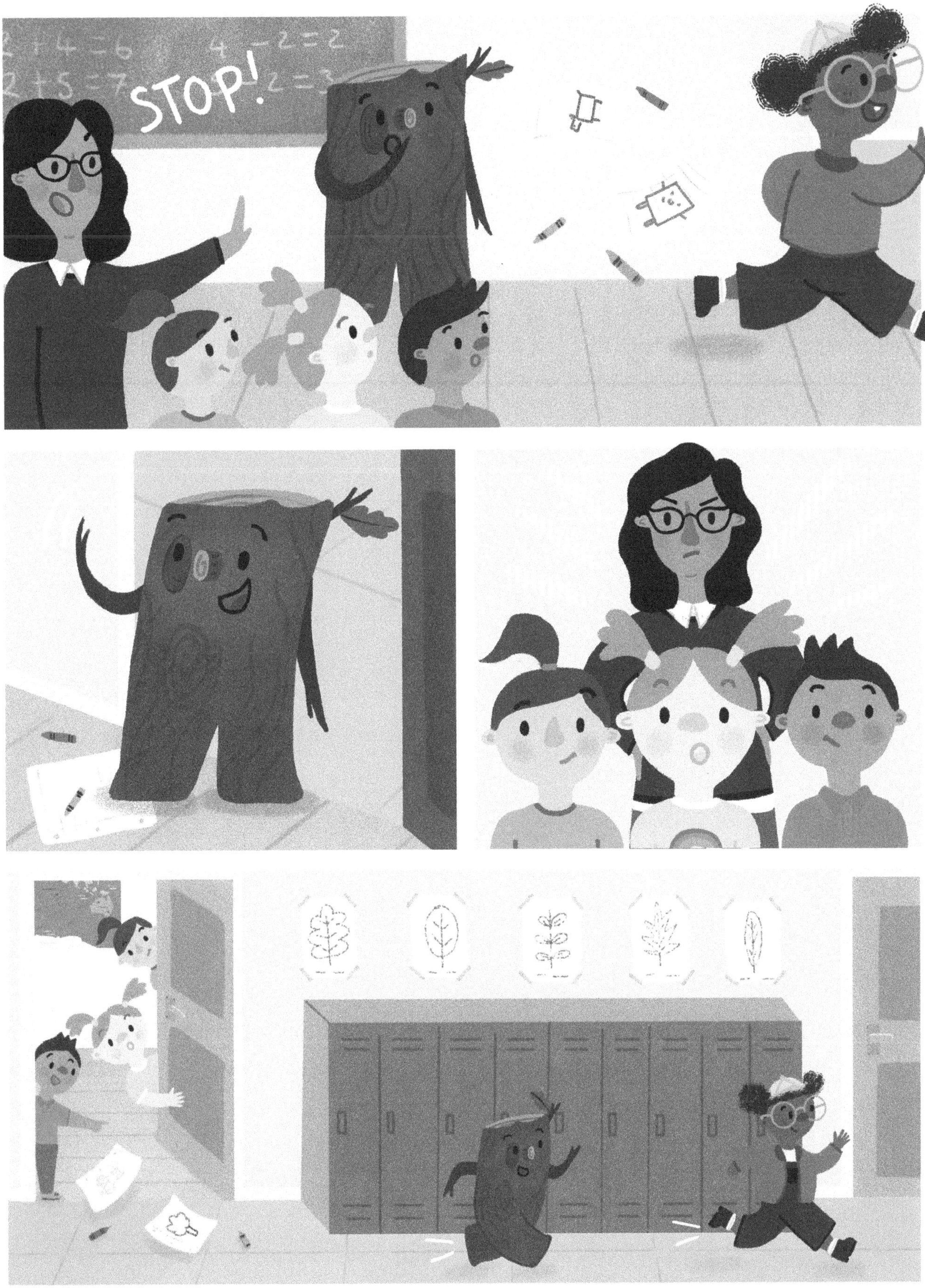
2 + 4 = 6
4 - 2 = 2
STOP!

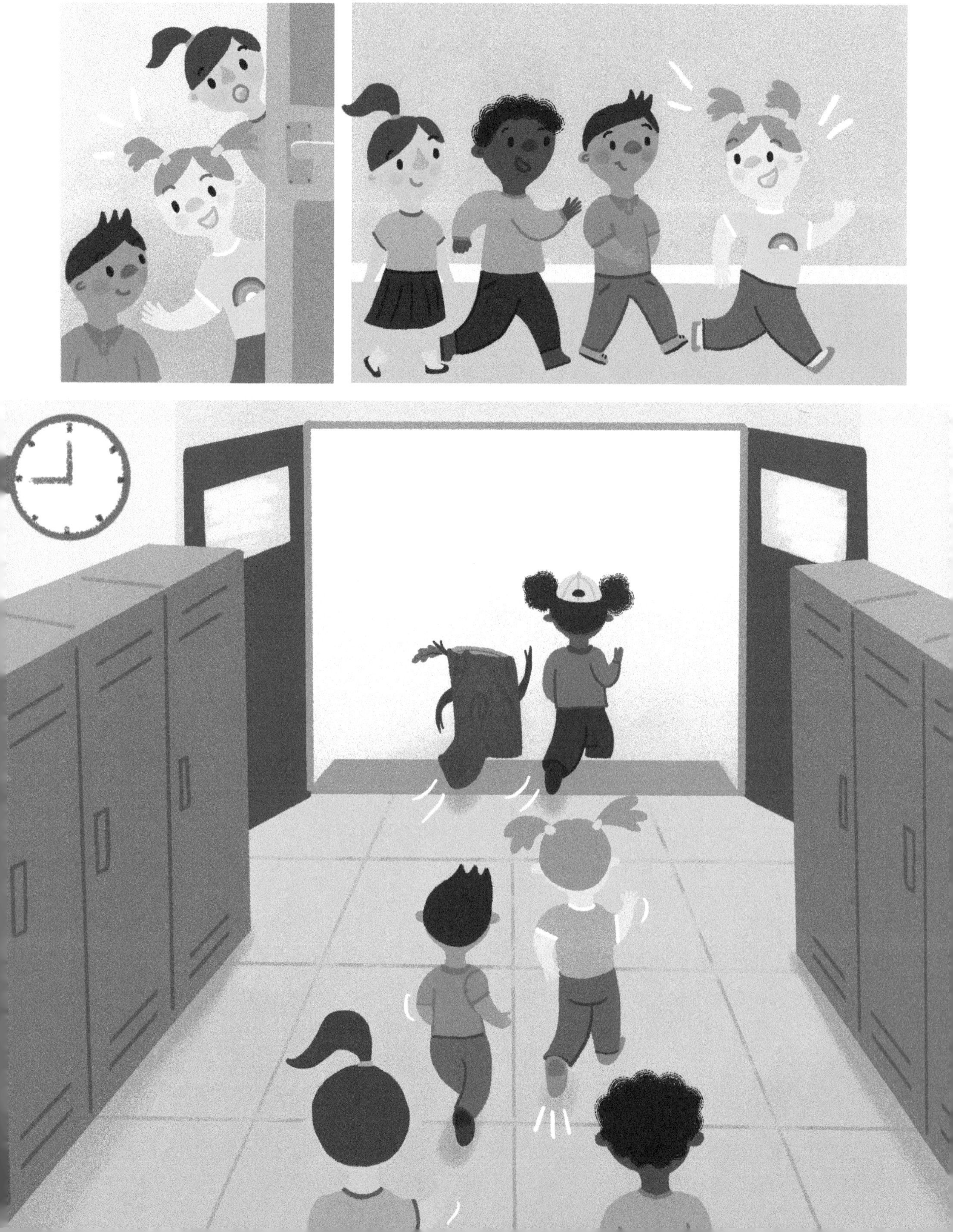

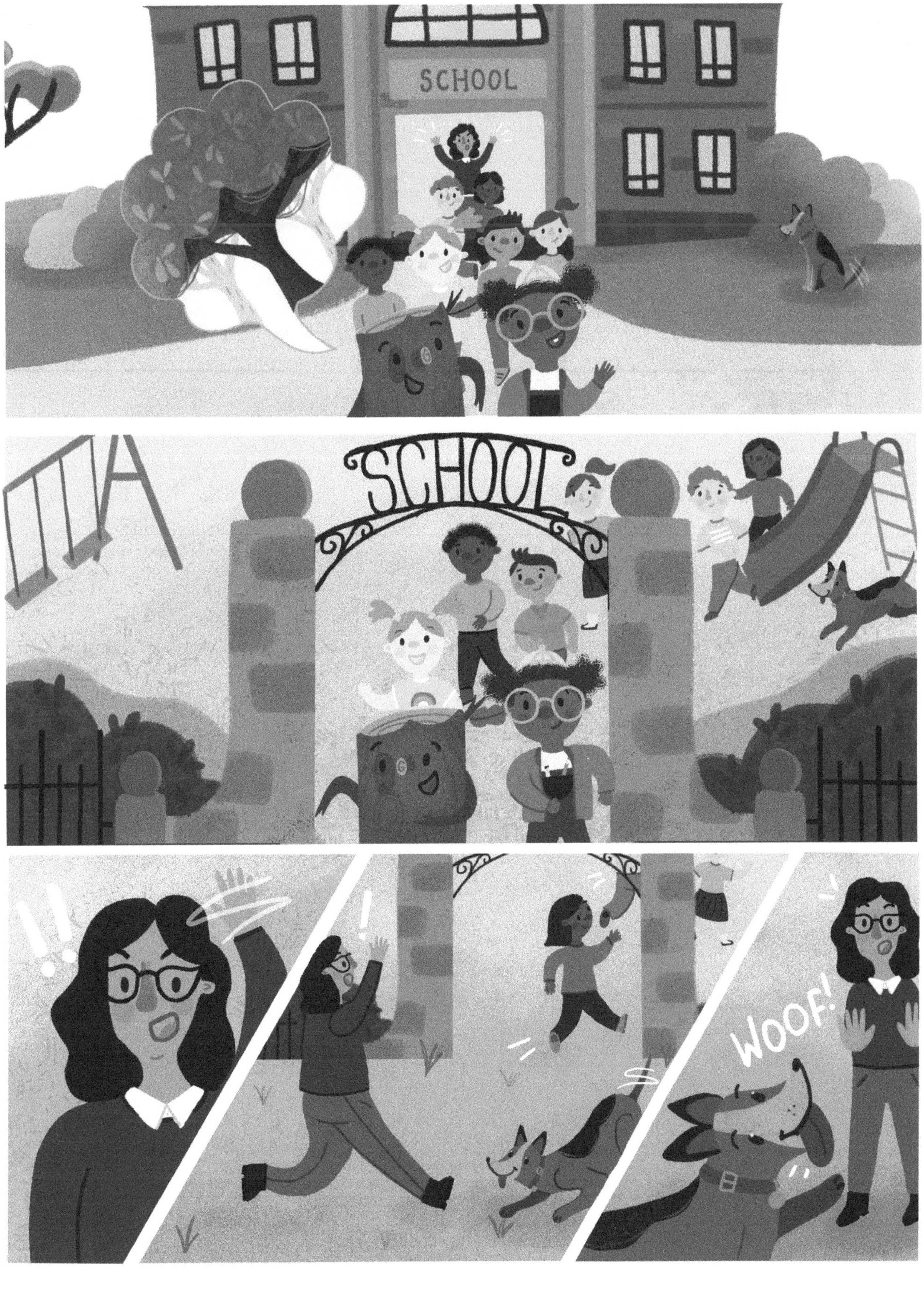
SCHOOL
SCHOOL
WOOF!

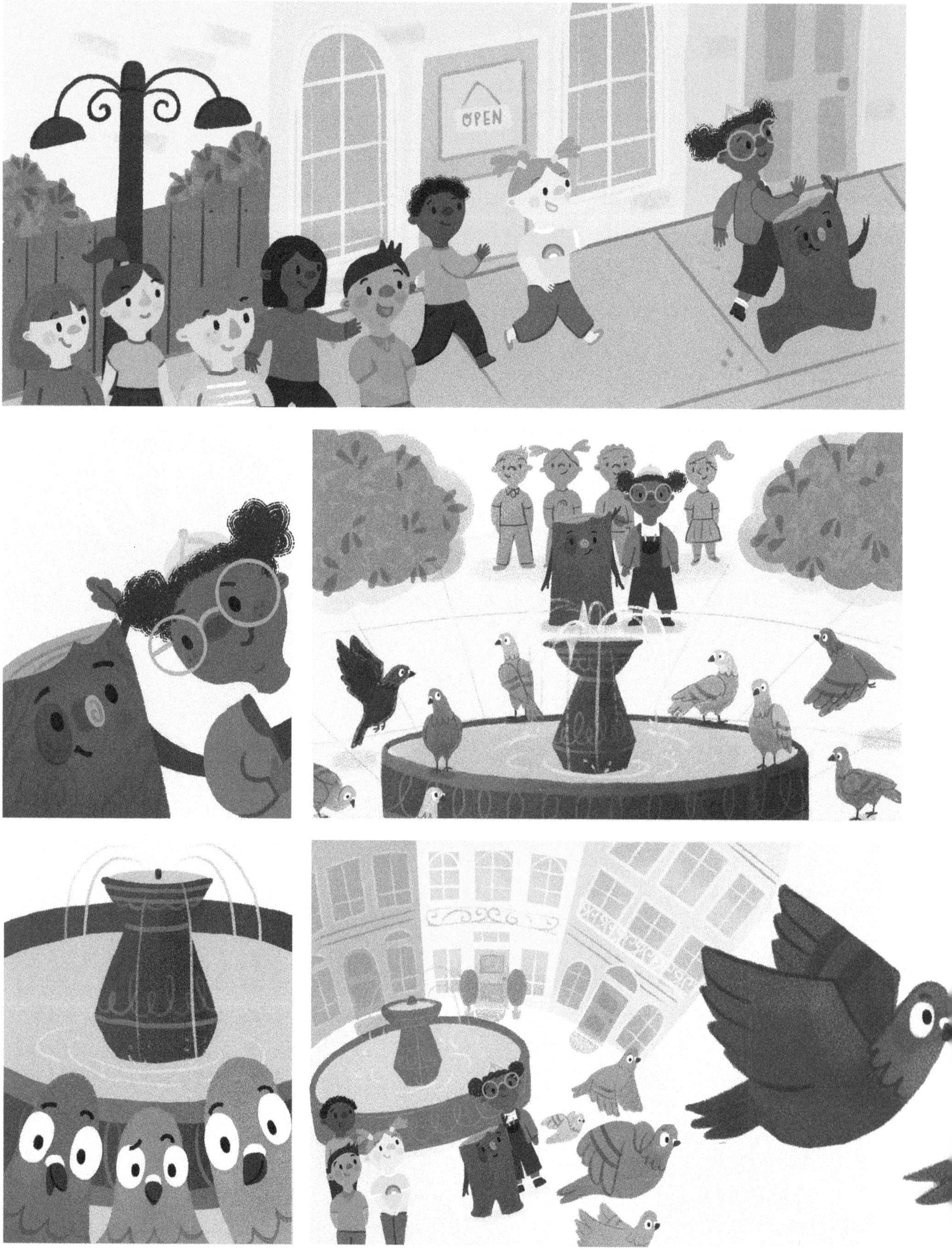
OPEN

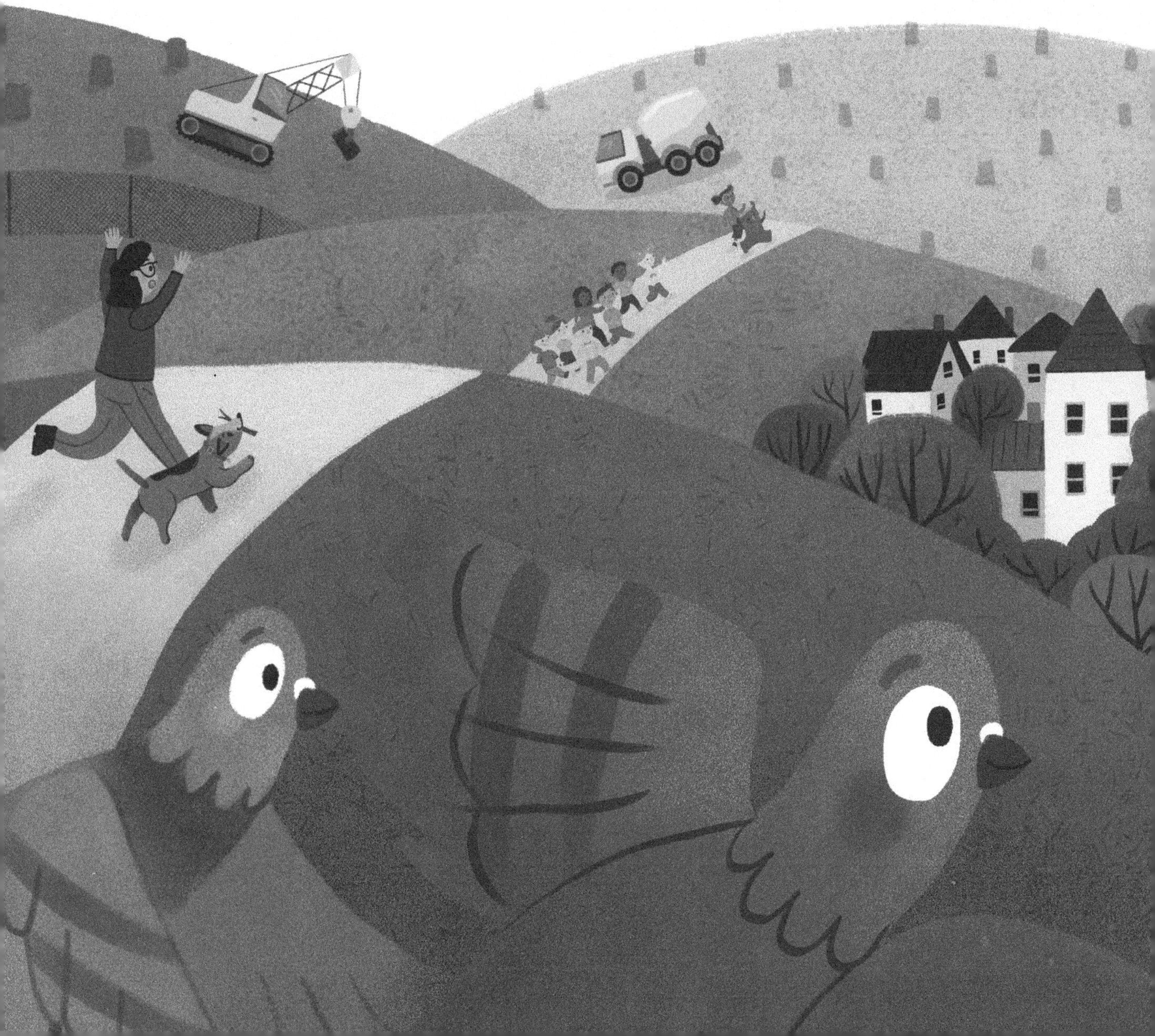

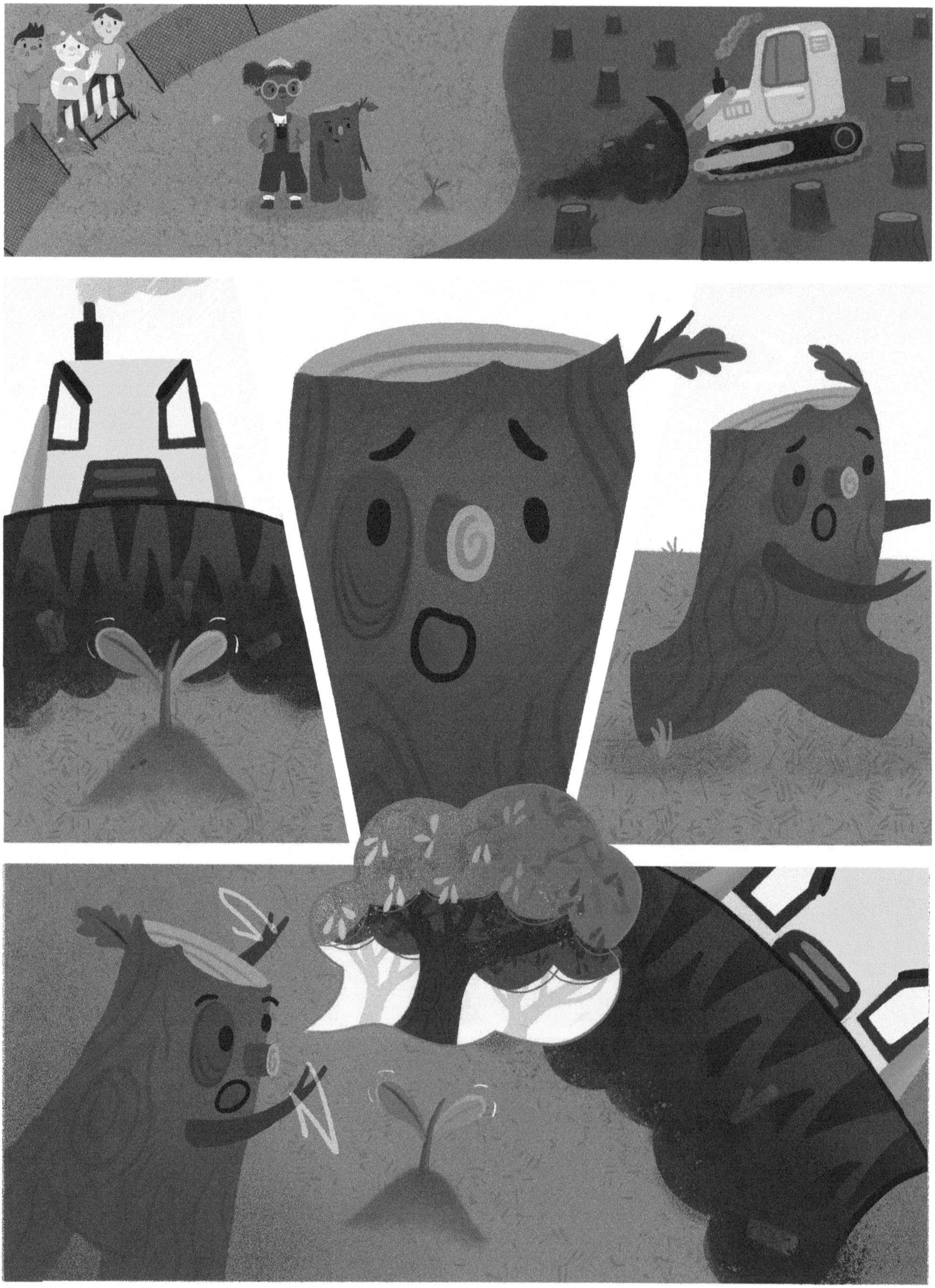

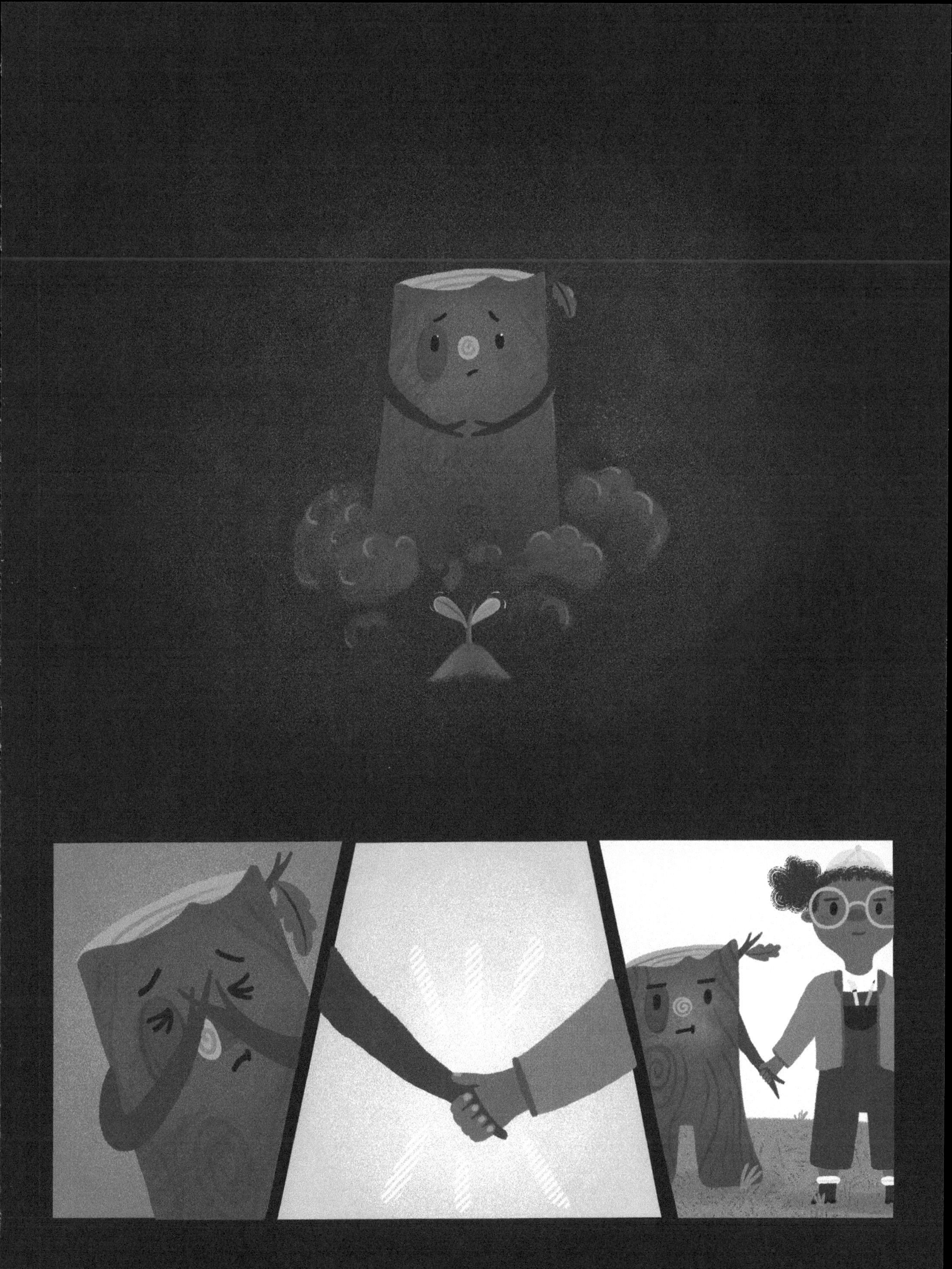

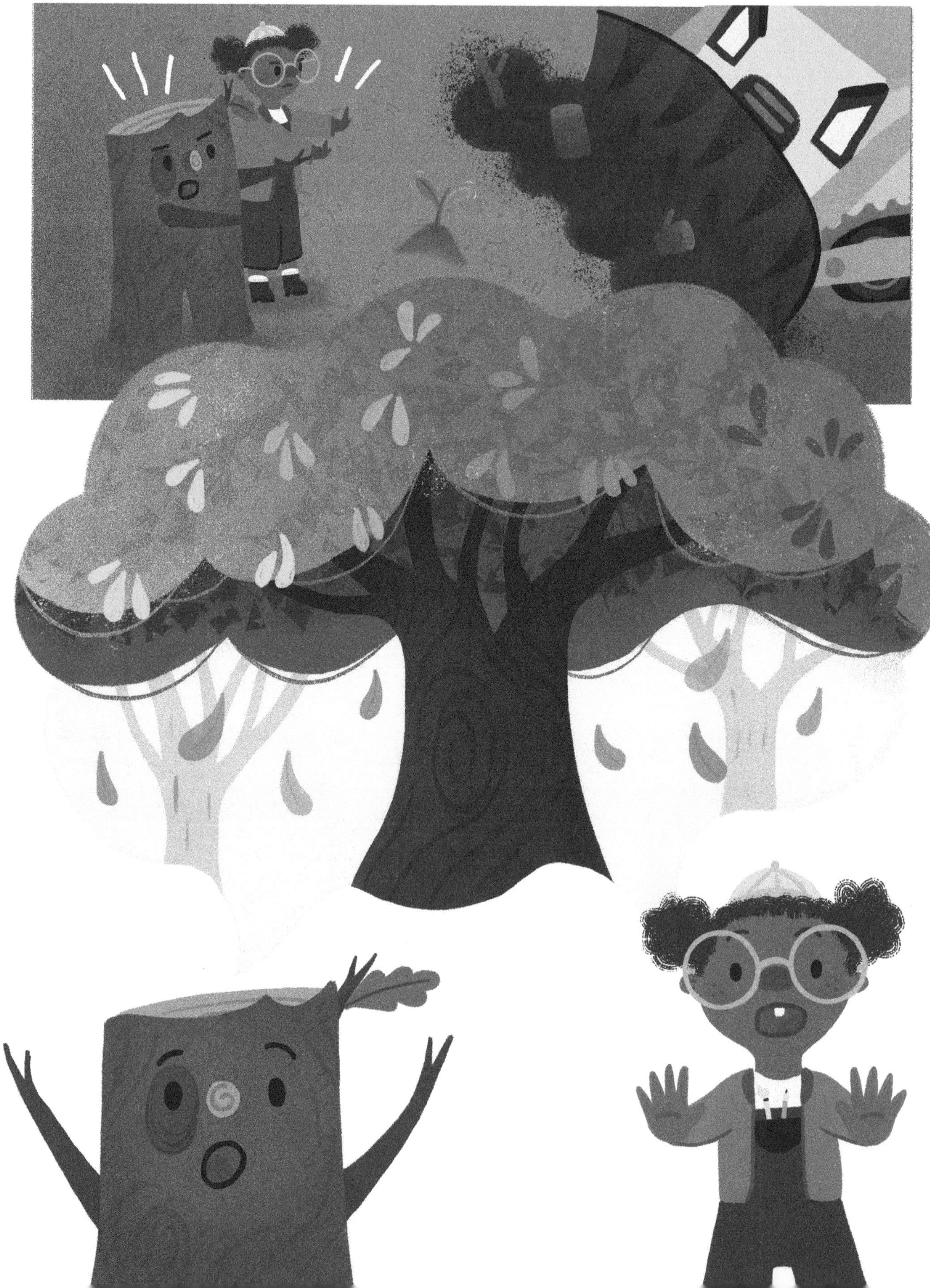

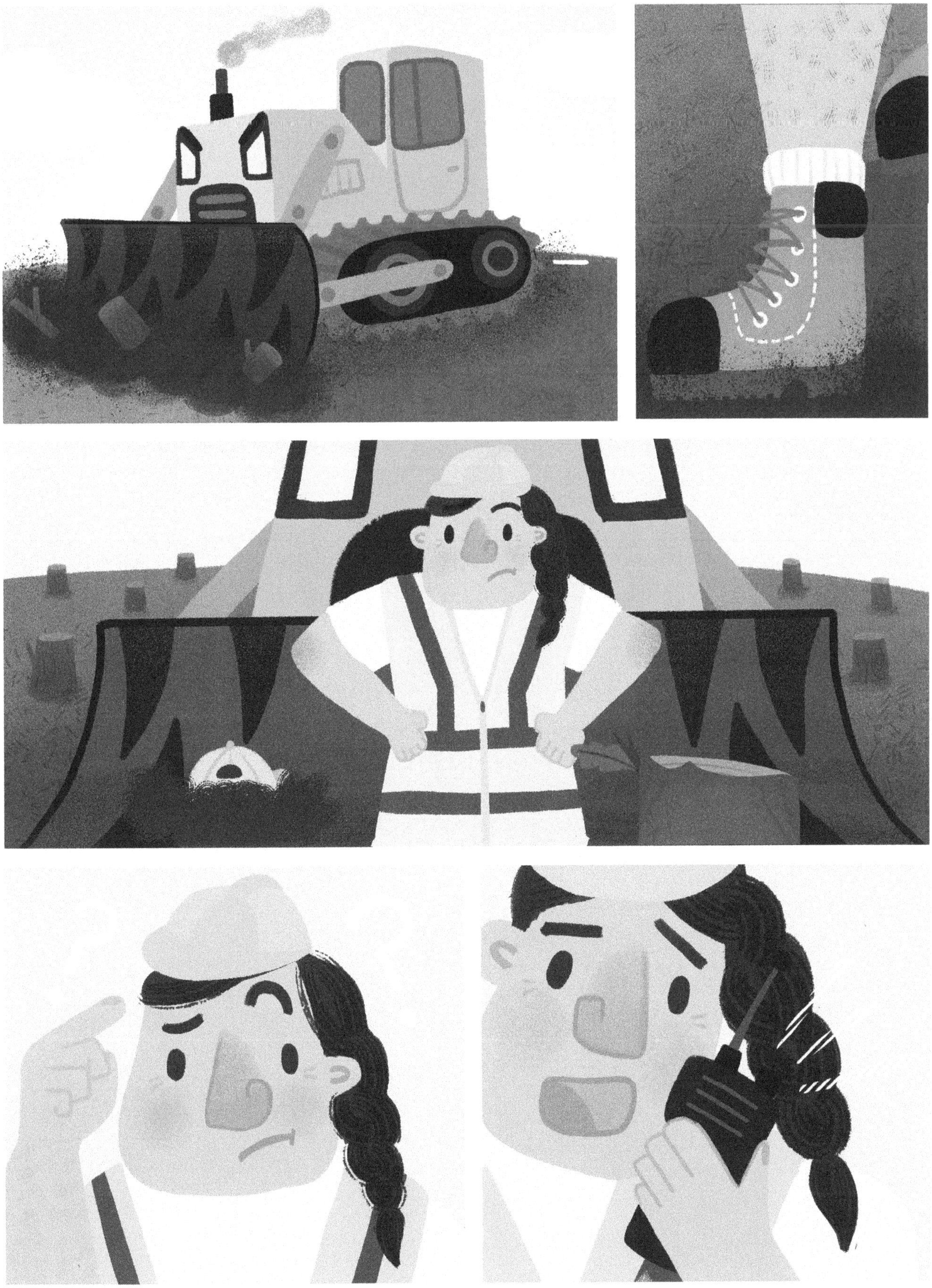

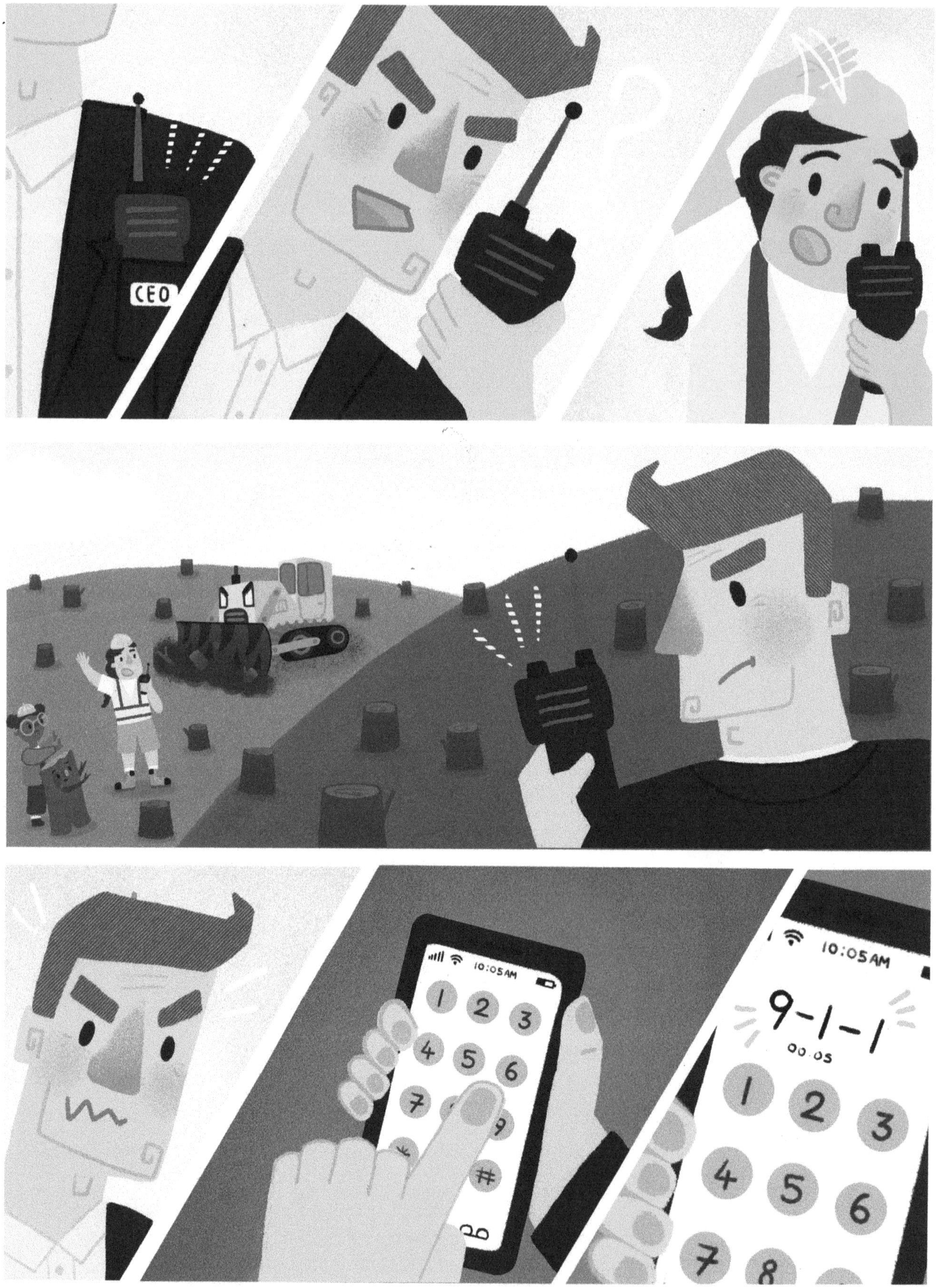
CEO
10:05AM
10:05AM
9-1-1
00:05

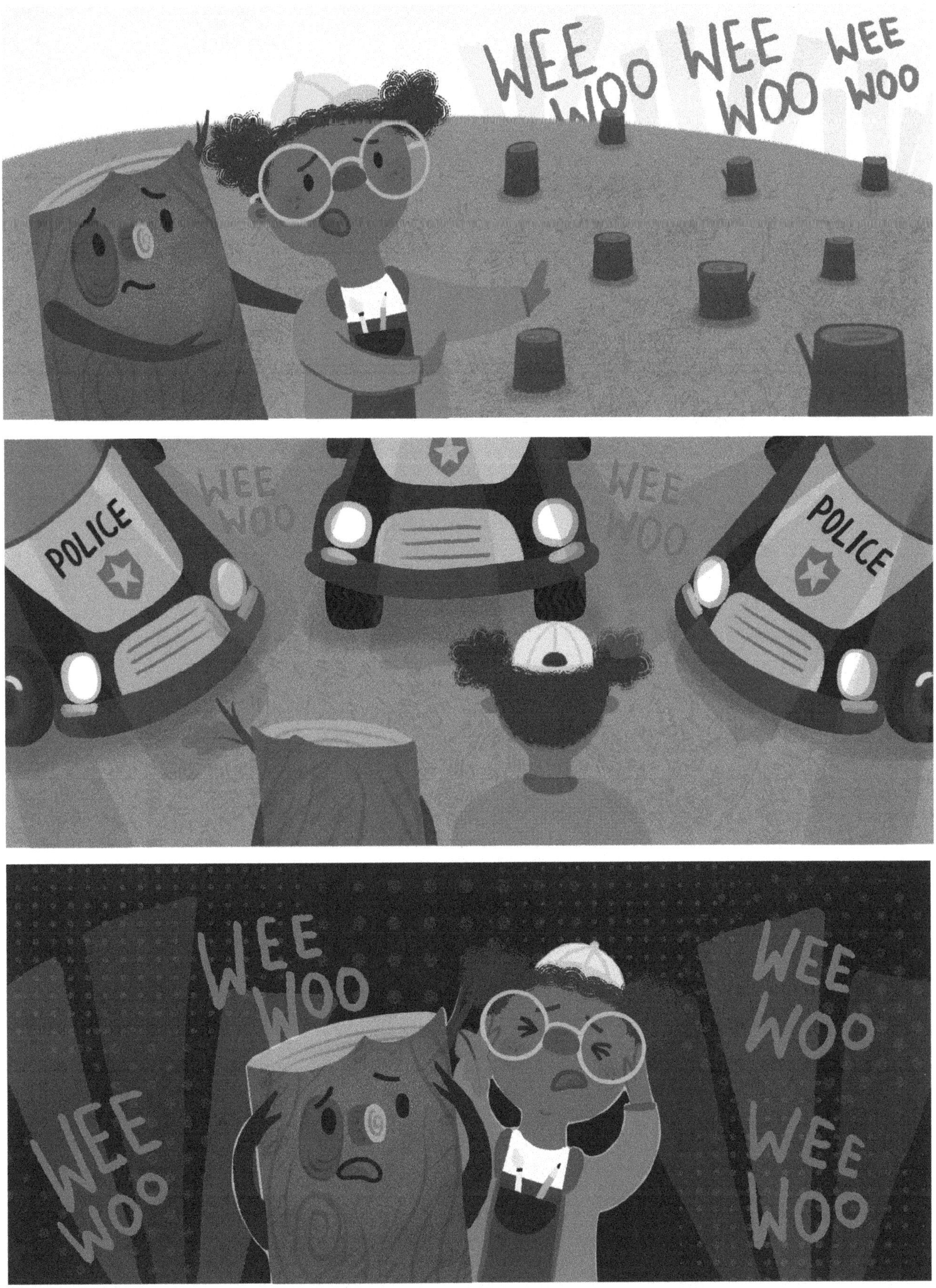
WEE WOO
WEE WOO
WEE WOO
POLICE
WEE WOO
WEE WOO
POLICE
WEE WOO
WEE WOO
WEE WOO
WEE WOO

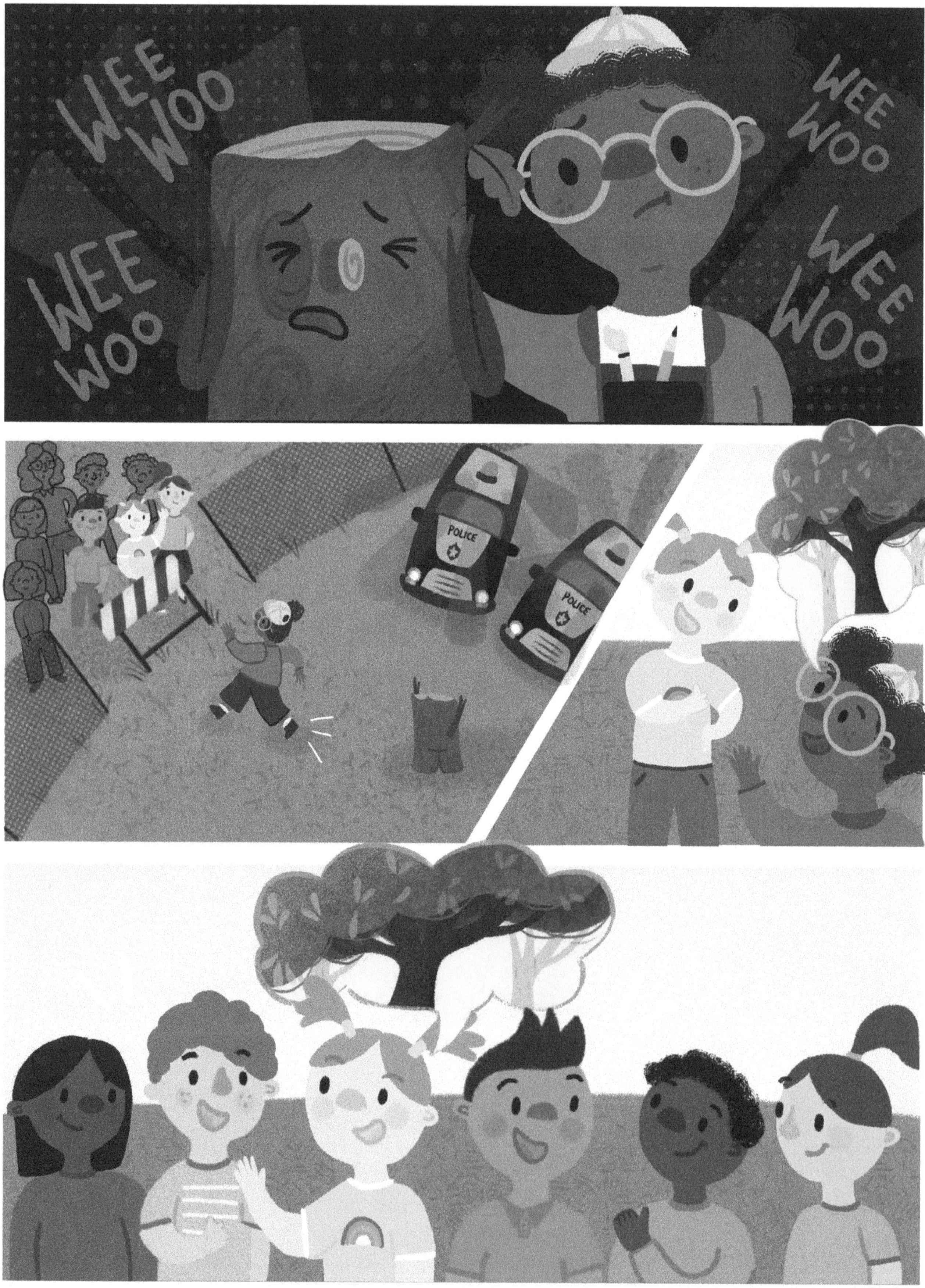
WEE WOO
WEE WOO
WEE WOO
WEE WOO
POLICE
POLICE

NEWS
NEWS

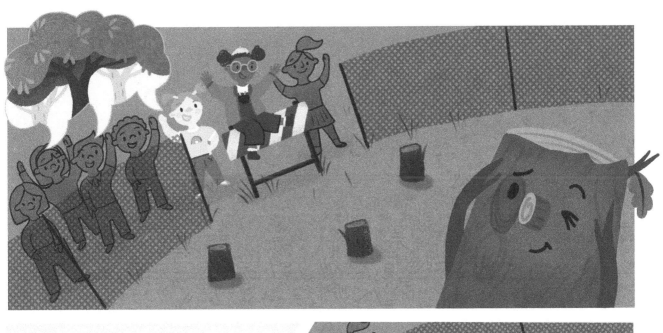

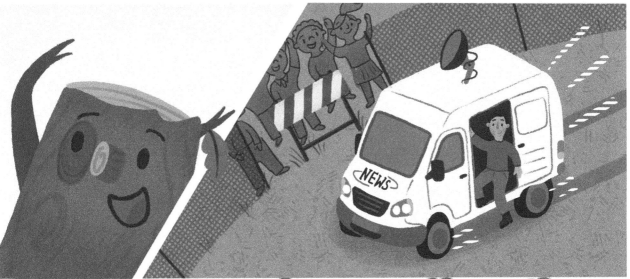

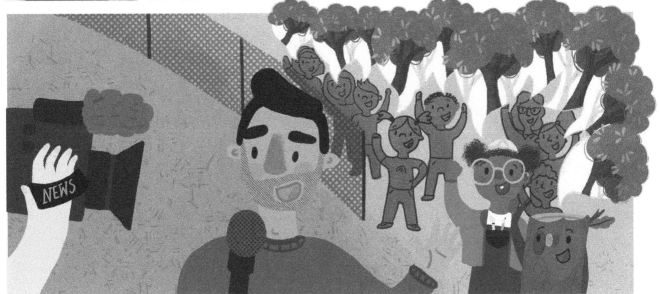

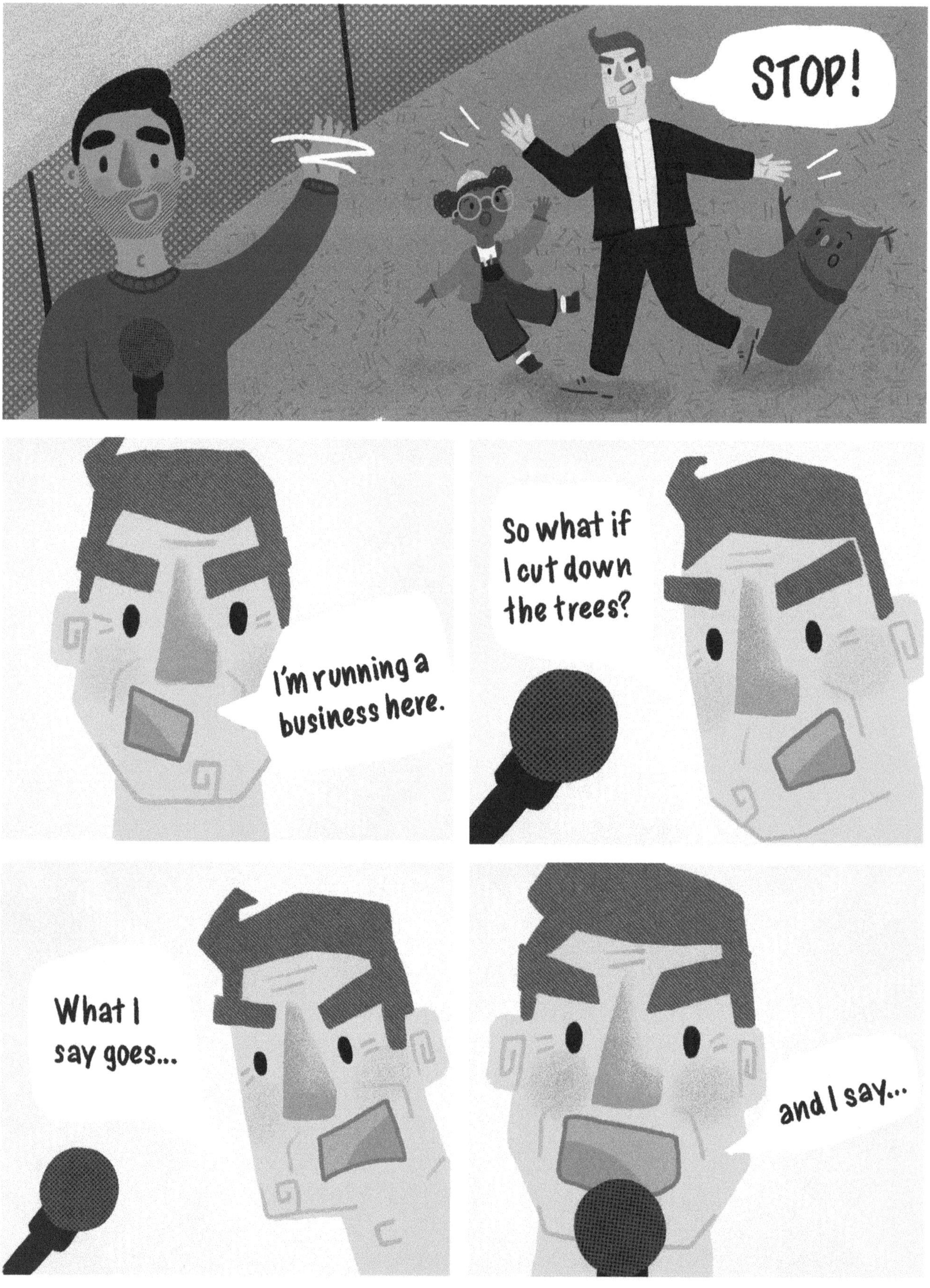
STOP!
I'm running a business here.
So what if I cut down the trees?
What I say goes...
and I say...

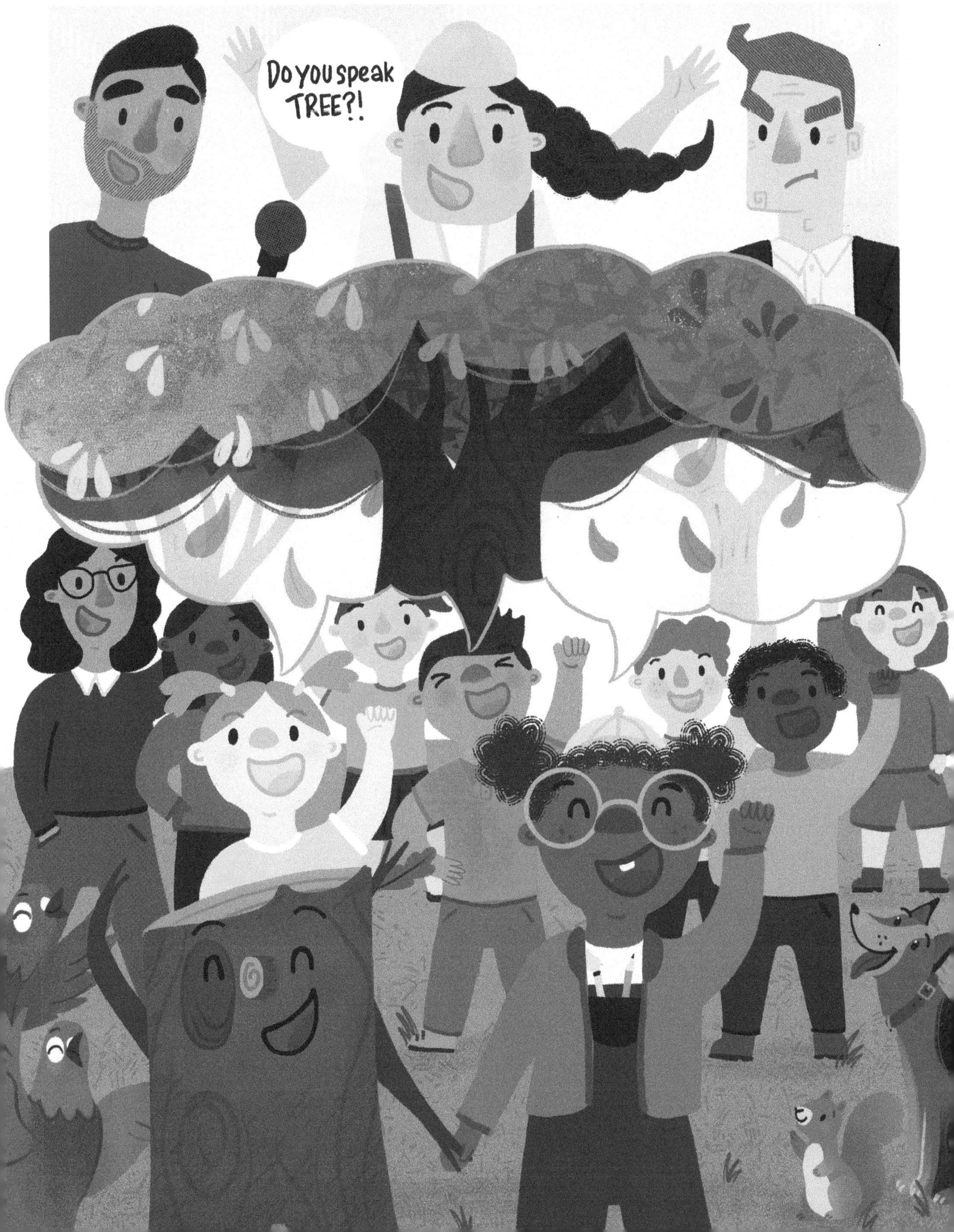
Do you speak TREE?!

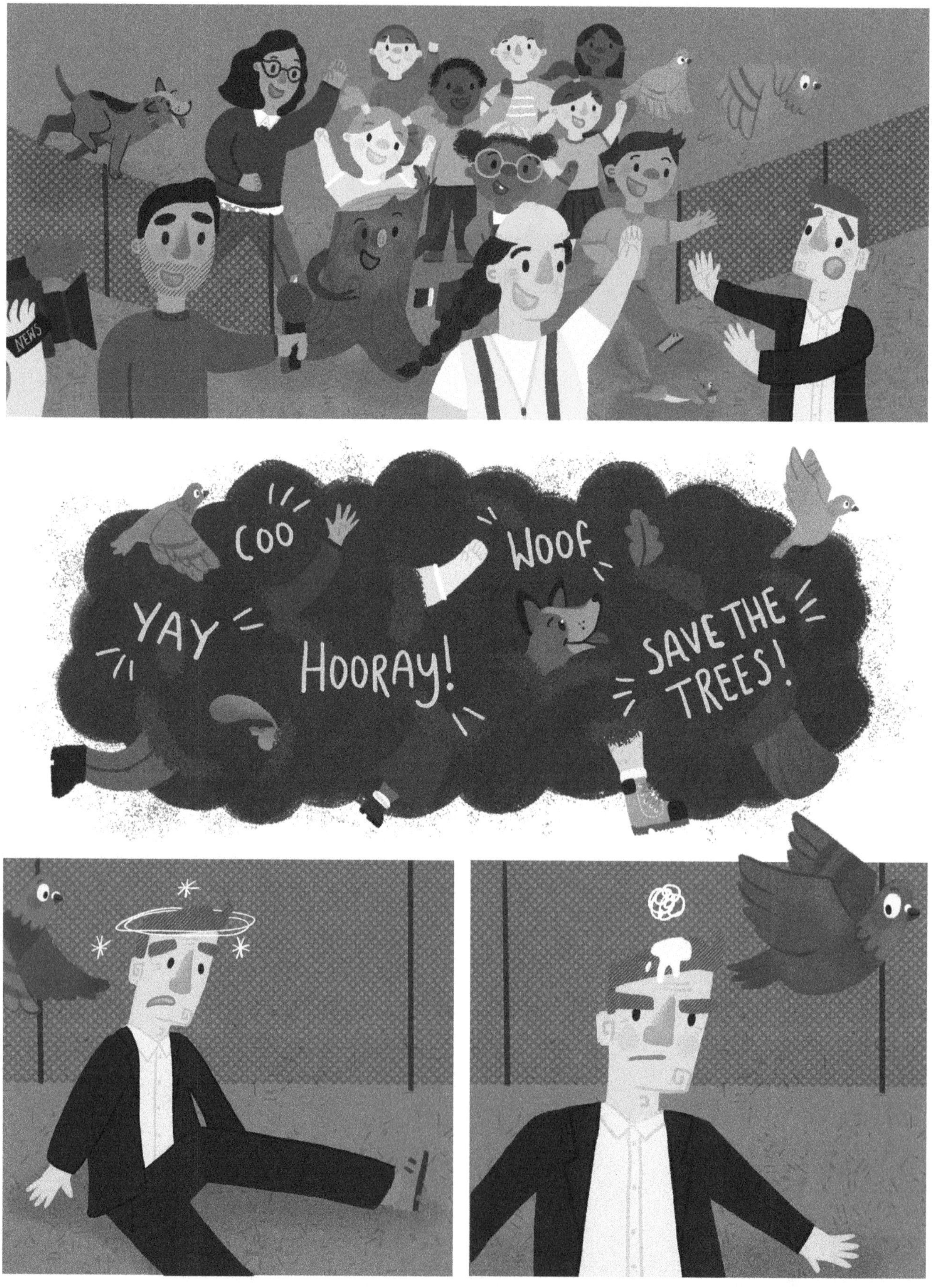
NEWS
COO
WOOF
YAY
HOORAY!
SAVE THE TREES!

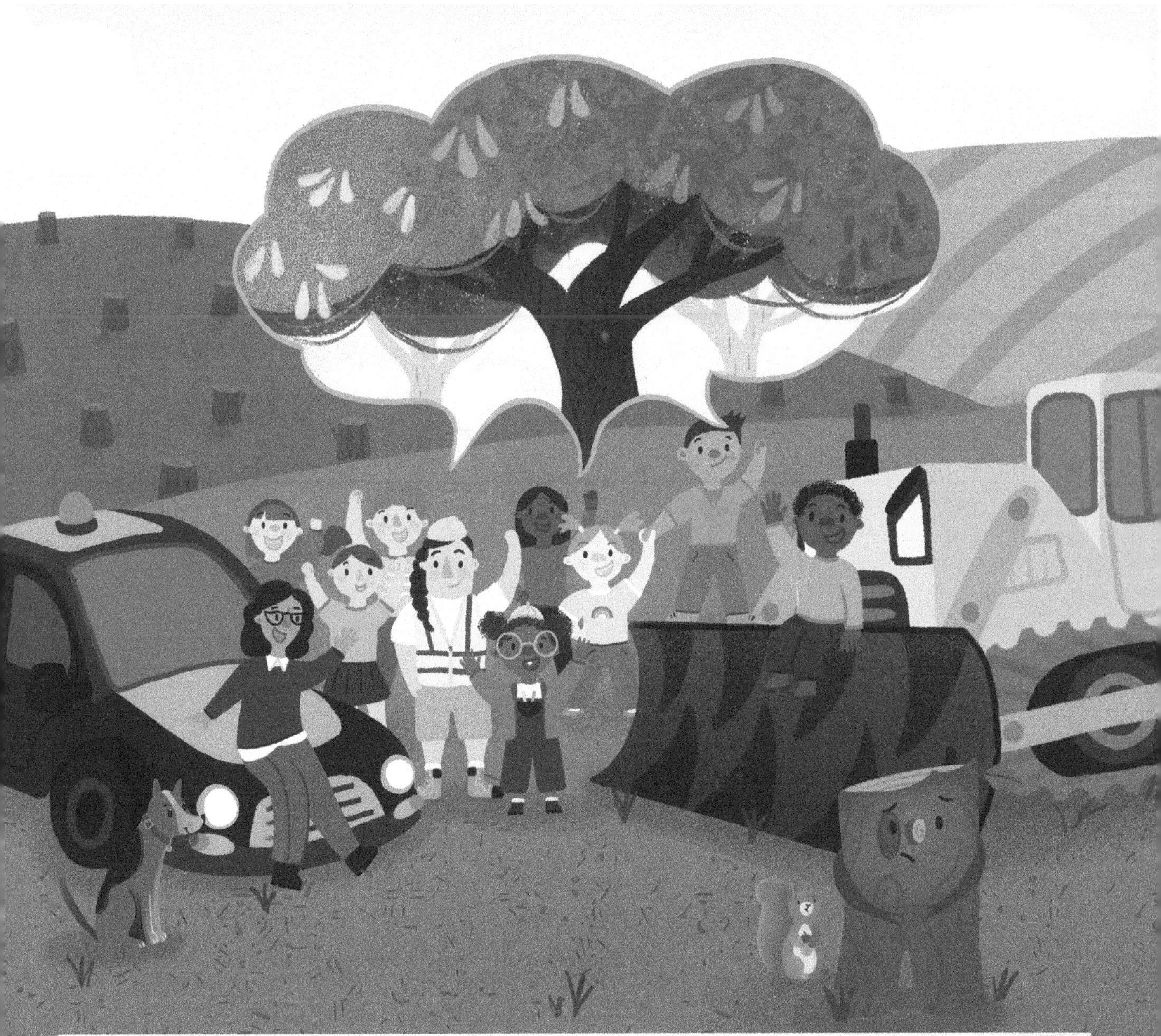
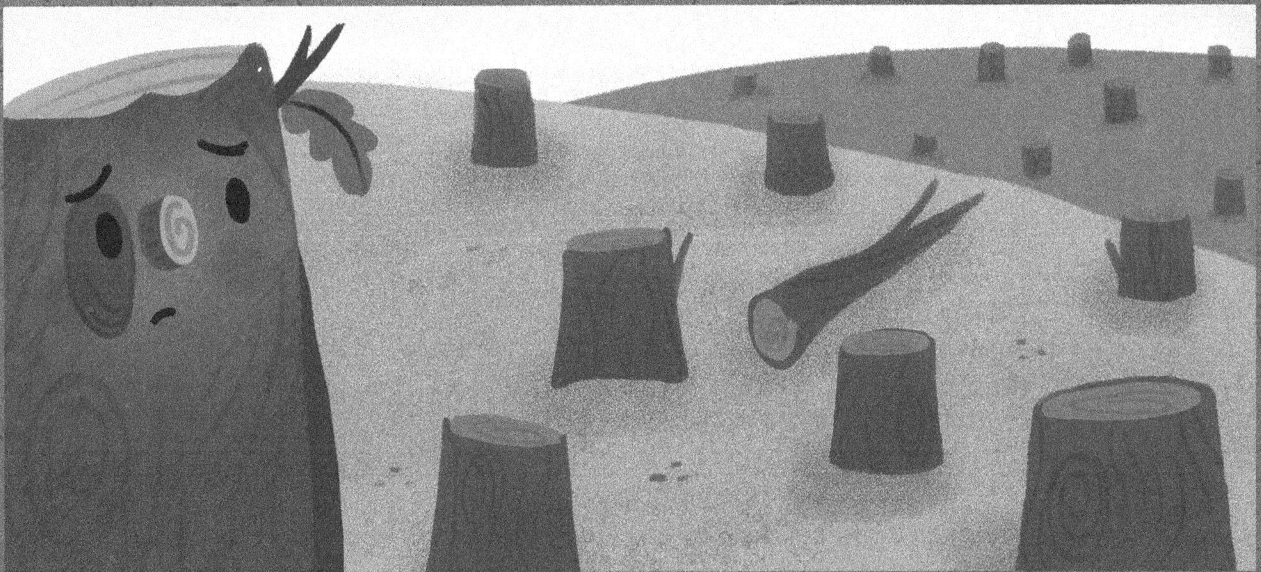

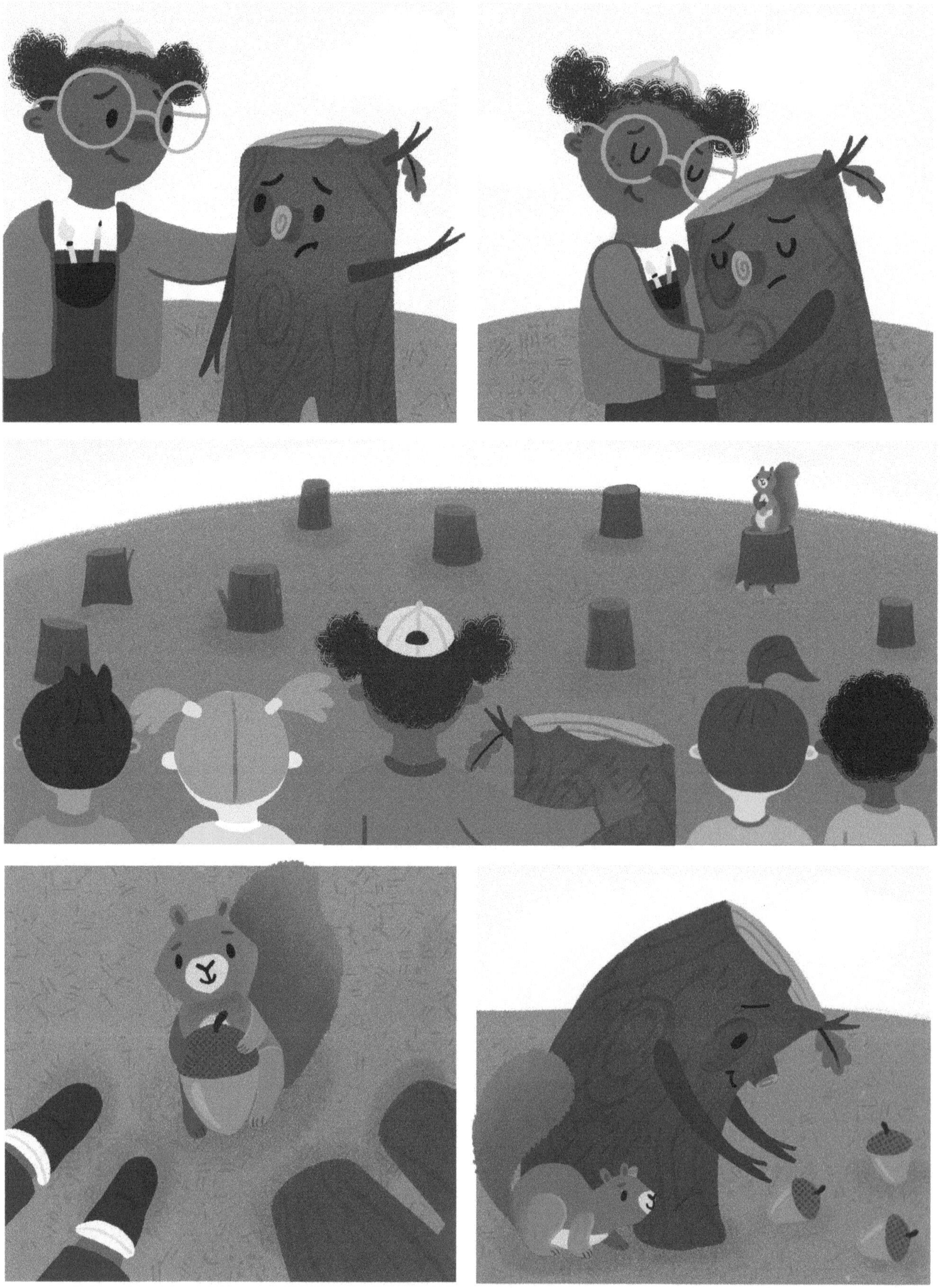

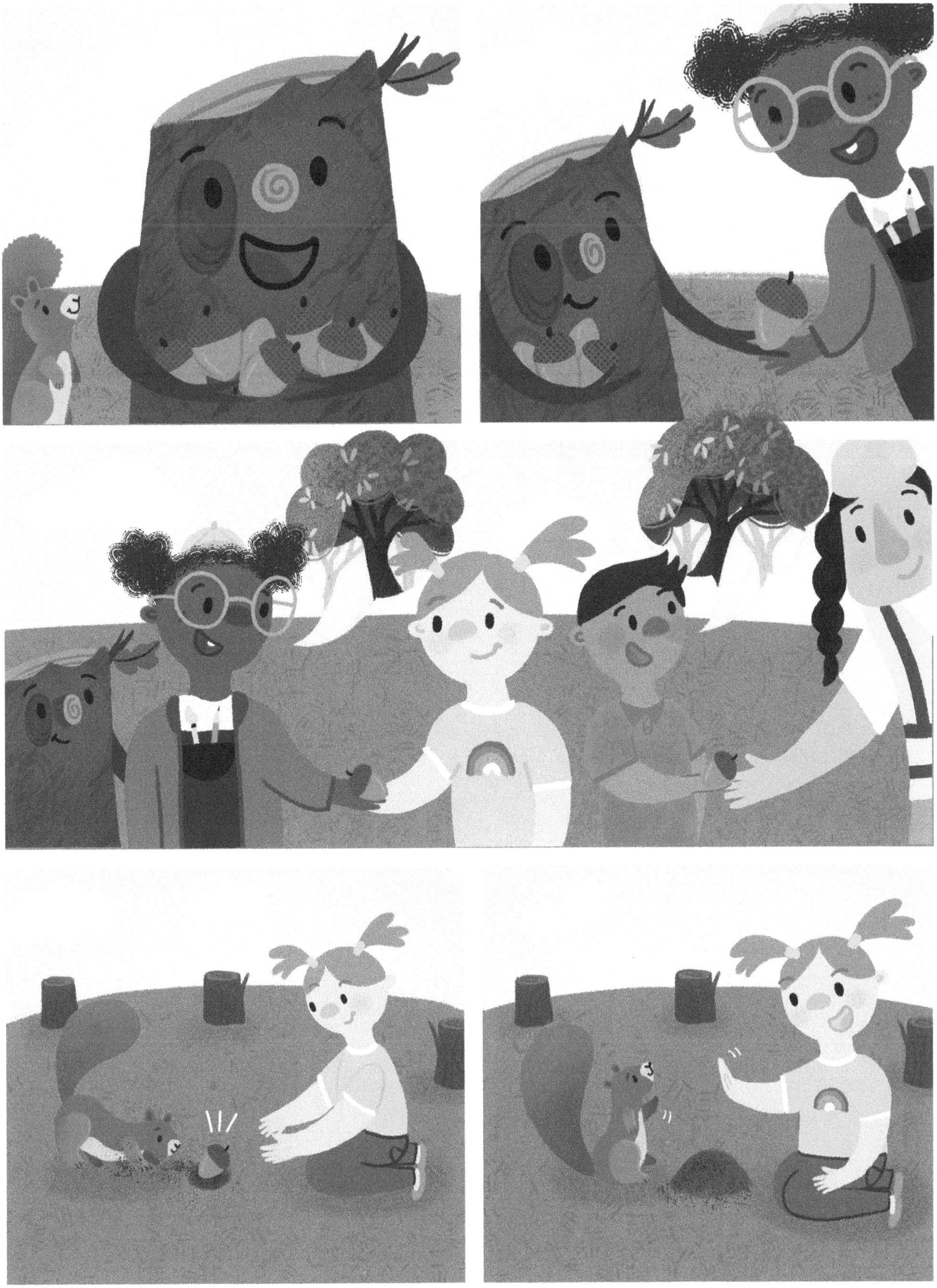

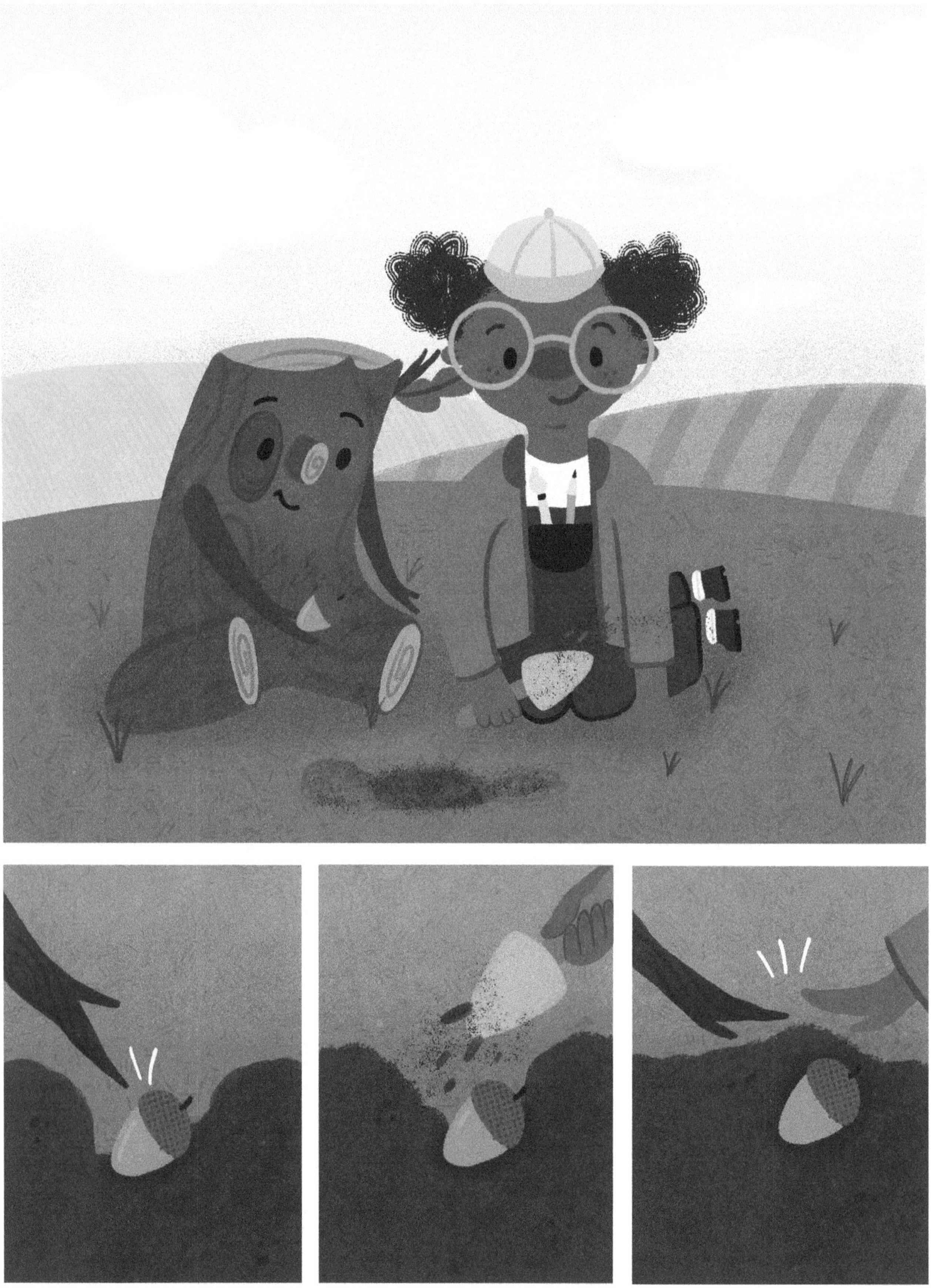

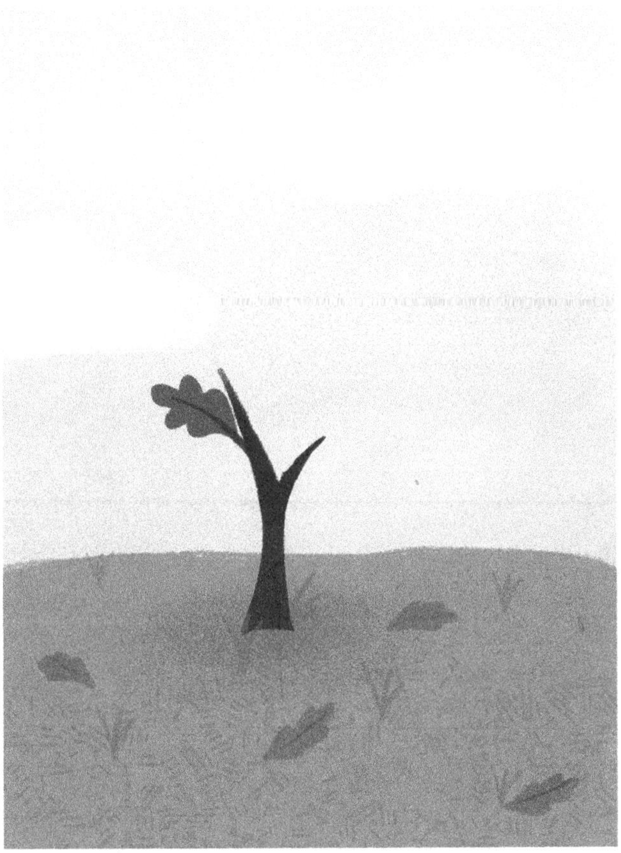

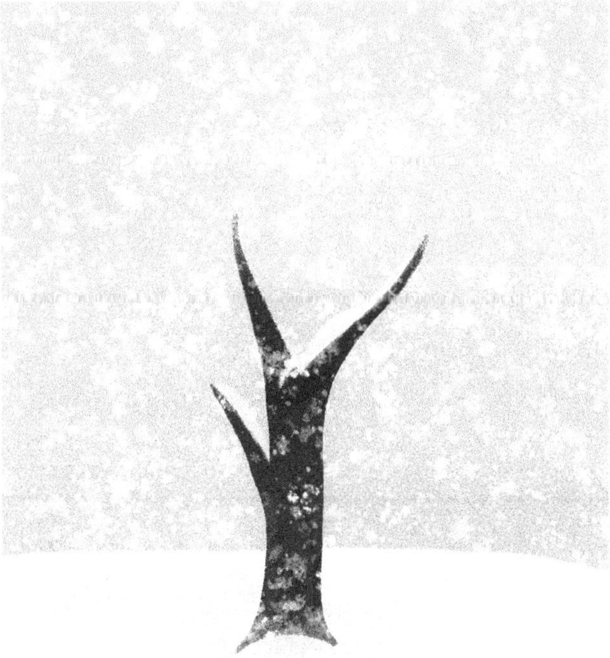

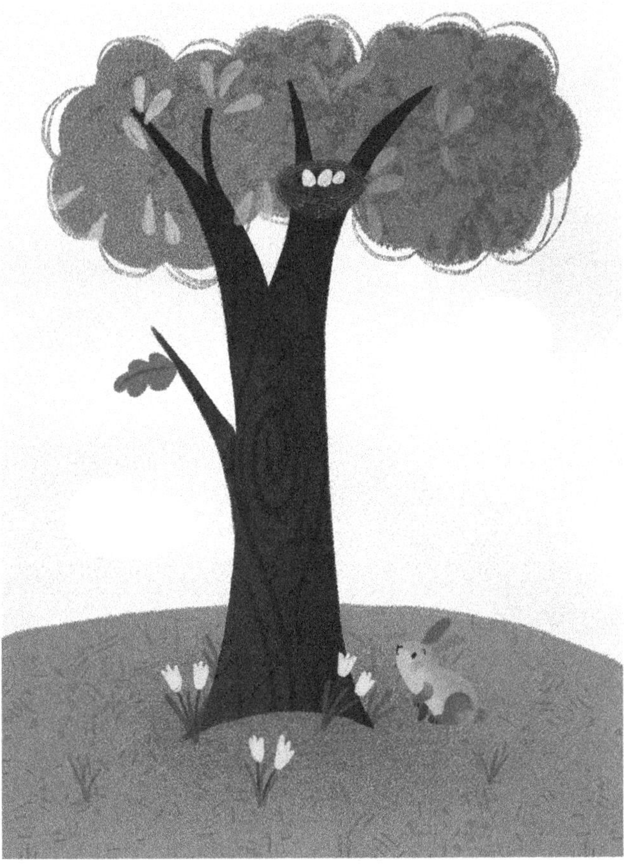

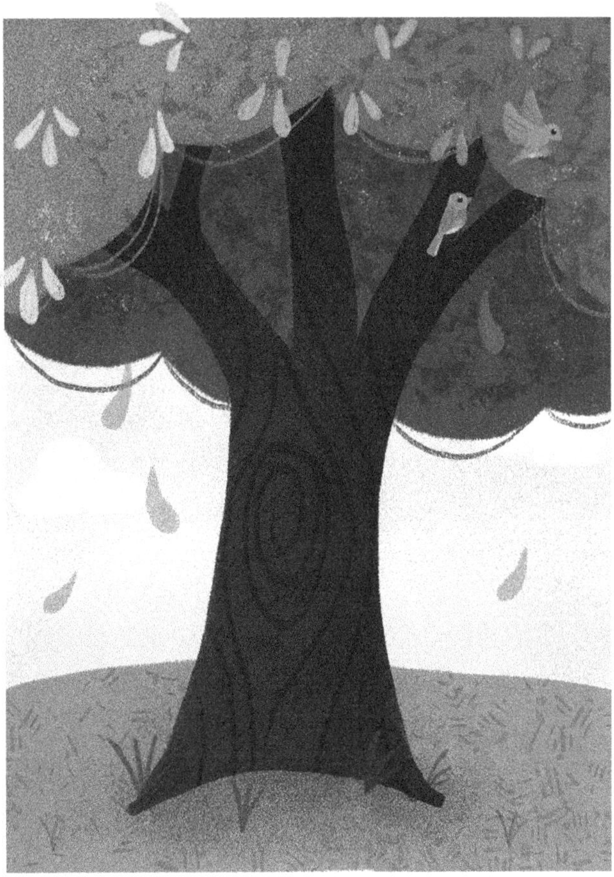

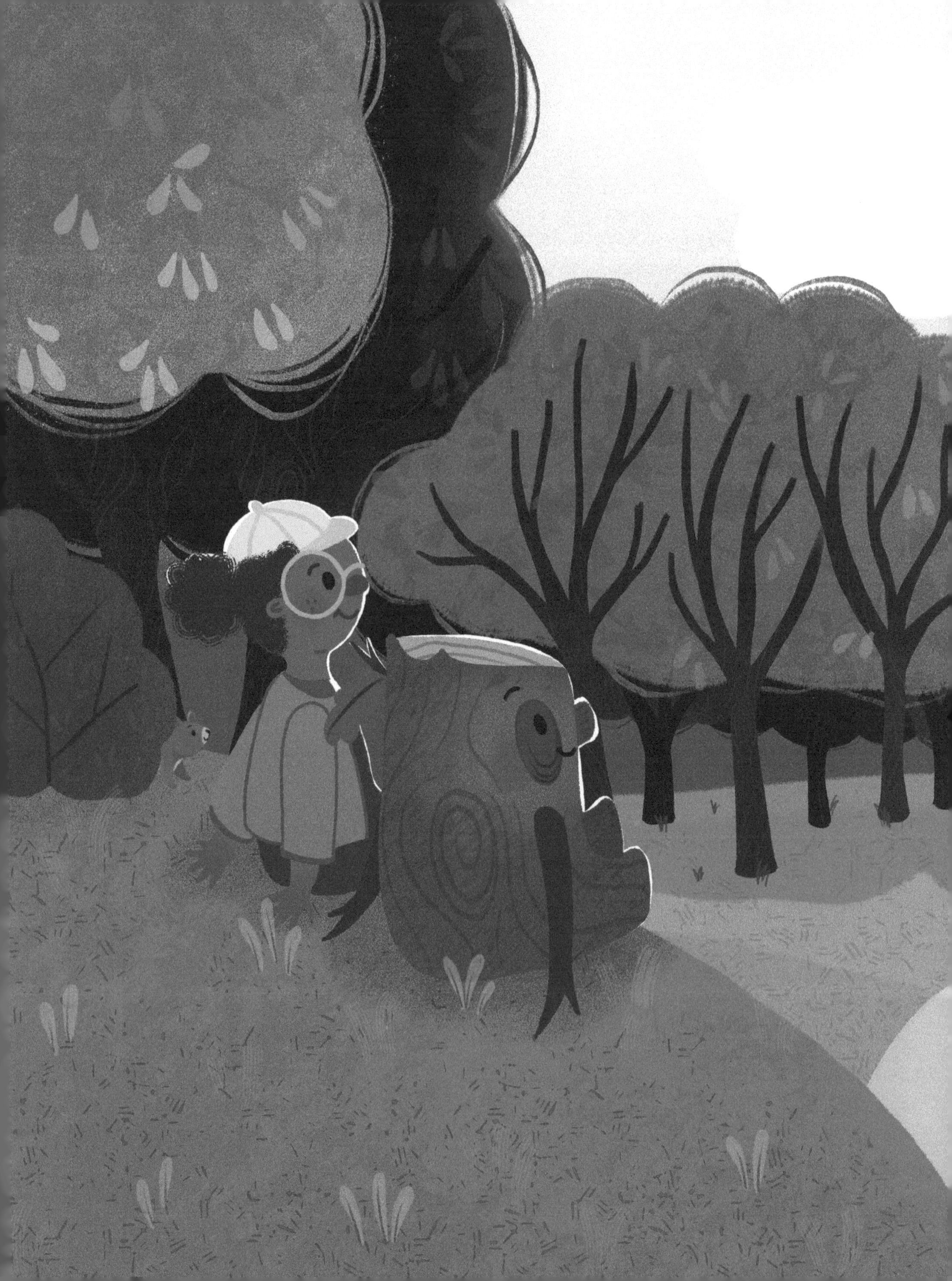

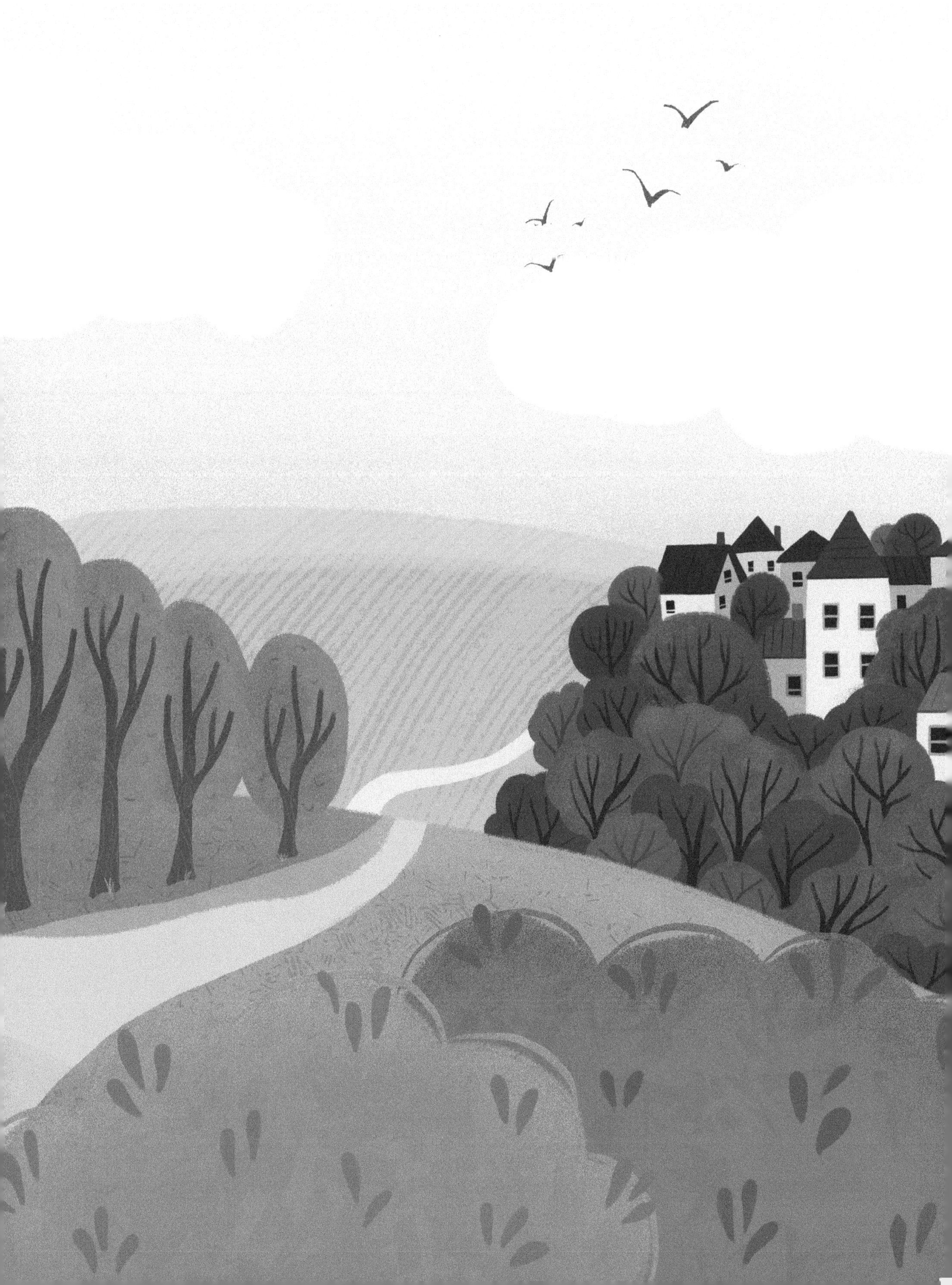

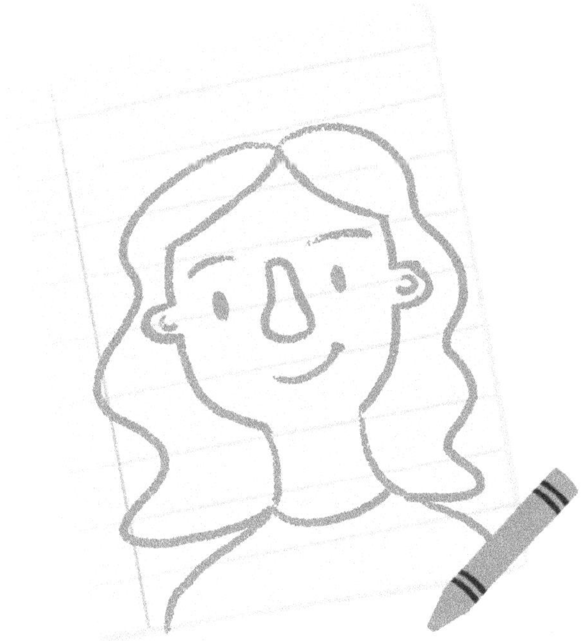

Josiane Vlitos

(illustrator) Josiane is an illustrator hailing from Vancouver, BC. When she's not drawing, you can find her with her nose in a book or her head in the clouds.

Josh Oaktree

(writer) Josh is the managing director and founder of Oak Tree Comics. He feels most at home atop a mountain, unicycle, or tree limb.

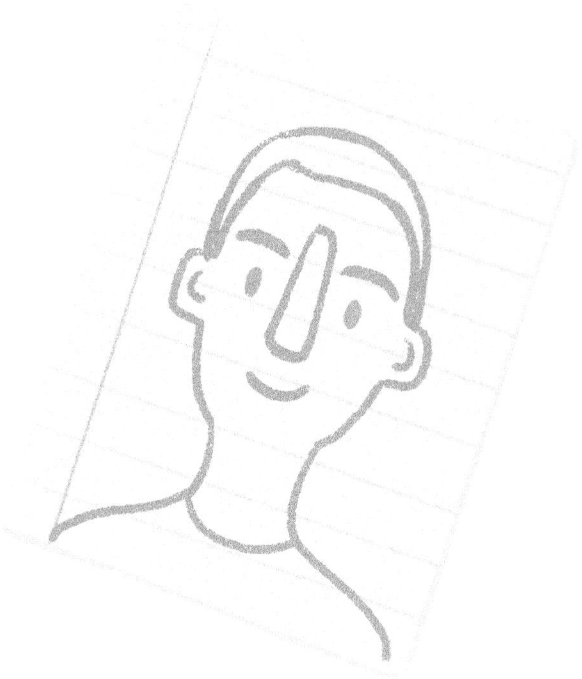

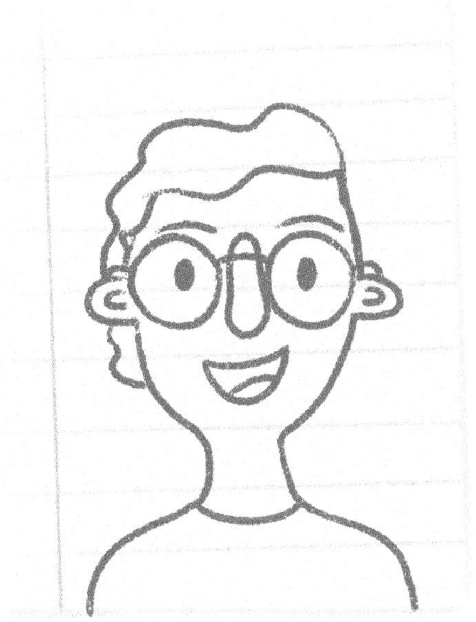

Amelia Boscov

(creative director) Amelia oversees the development of original stories at Oak Tree Comics. She loves working on artistic projects in print, on screen, and with yarn.

Now that you've read *Do You Speak Tree?*, we would love to learn how you #speaktree.

You can share your drawings, photos, poems, videos, and more with us @OakTree_Comics. Make sure to tag us and use the hashtag #speaktree.

Visit us on the web to download a free PDF of discussion questions for the book to use in your classroom or at home: oaktreecomics.com/speak-tree

Thanks to the Vlitos, Boscov, and Aichenbaum families, whose love and support planted the seed to create this book.

Thanks to the communities on Facebook and Instagram whose enthusiasm provided the sunshine for our story to grow.

And thanks to Ethan Jacobs, Will Piekos, Tom Ladeau, Randall Brown, Janine McDonald, and Shannon Barrett who, through their time and energies, helped Oak Tree Comics blossom in its first year.

Visit us on the web: oaktreecomics.com

Follow us on Instagram and Facebook @OakTree_Comics

Managing director and founder: Josh Oaktree
Creative director: Amelia Boscov

Copyright © 2021 Oak Tree Comics, LLC

All Rights Reserved. For information about permission to reproduce selections from this book, direct inquiries to info@oaktreecomics.com

Your book purchase plants a tree. For every book sold, Oak Tree Comics donates a dollar to One Tree Planted, a non-profit 501(c)3.

Library of Congress Control Number: 2021906765

ISBN: 978-1-954754-02-7 (hardcover)
ISBN: 978-1-954754-03-4 (e-book)
ISBN: 978-1-954754-01-0 (paperback)

COMING SOON!

ART & OAKIE ask:

DO YOU SPEAK BEAR?

OAK-TREE COMICS

CPSIA information can be obtained
at www.ICGtesting.com
Printed in the USA
LVHW071505020521
686267LV00014B/1623